LOVE'S DESIGN

LOVE'S DESIGN

•

Jillian Dagg

AVALON BOOKS
NEW YORK

c.1

© Copyright 2000 by Jillian Dagg
Library of Congress Catalog Card Number: 00-100840
ISBN 0-8034-9425-4
Published by Thomas Bouregy & Co., Inc.
160 Madison Avenue, New York, NY 10016

PRINTED IN THE UNITED STATES OF AMERICA
ON ACID-FREE PAPER
BY HADDON CRAFTSMEN, BLOOMSBURG, PENNSYLVANIA

For Marilyn & Brian Wilde
25 years

Chapter One

On a bleak Monday morning in February, with snow blowing horizontally across the little ski community of Ashton Heights, New York, Lori Fenton wanted to put her sleek silver car in reverse and return home.

On Friday, Ken Randall and Peter Rhodes, her bosses at Randall & Rhodes, Architects, had ruined her weekend when they called her into Ken's office.

"A new man is starting on Monday," Ken had told her. "His name is Sean Matheson. He's coming from a big Manhattan architectural firm." Ken, stocky and dark-haired, had glanced at his lanky partner, Peter, at that point.

Peter had adjusted his striped tie. "Lori, we believe he will complement Randall & Rhodes. He's going to

1

be working on the Hinton Ski Lodge and Resort with you."

Lori had grumbled. Not to Ken. Not to Peter. She had grumbled to her mother and father, Jack and Alice Fenton, and her girlfriend, Susan Hall. "Hinton Ski Lodge was my project, my first major job, and now I have to share it."

Her builder father, a friend of Ken's, had tried to console her. "Lori, you're only two years out of college. Ken knows what he's doing."

"I haven't had a chance to prove myself yet, Dad. Hinton's was going to be that chance."

Pretty, red-headed Susan, always on the lookout for a man, had batted her eyes and said, "Maybe he'll be a hunk."

"I don't want a hunk, Susan. This is *my* job, *my* career. I feel like I've been demoted. Both partners are more or less telling me that I'm not capable of handling a big project by myself, so they are bringing in a . . . a man."

"That's your main problem," Susan had said. "You resent that he's a man."

Lori drove her car through the snow into the parking lot of the brick century house. With the collar of her black wool coat up around her neck, she ran across the slippery asphalt and mounted the stone steps to the heavy oak door. Even though the wind tangled her long brown hair and lashed freezing air on to her skin, she hesitated at the brass door handle. She didn't want to go into work today. She wanted things to stay the way they had been. But when she had mentioned that to her mother yesterday, Alice had said, "Life isn't that way, Lori. Life has ups and downs."

Well, today was a definite down. A deep down.

Lori pulled on the door handle. The reception area was decorated with maroon carpet and cream walls. At the circular oak desk sat Mary Arnold, her silver upswept hair and black suit projecting the professional image Ken and Peter preferred in the front office.

"Terrible morning," Mary commented as she slit open an Express courier envelope with a silver letter opener.

Lori tossed her briefcase and purse onto a brocade visitor's chair, tucked her suede gloves into her pockets, and stamped the remaining few snowflakes from her booted feet on to the serviceable carpet. She began to unbutton her coat. "Terrible only half describes it."

Mary glanced down her nose over her reading glasses. "What's bitten you?"

"What do you think?"

Mary indicated the back offices with a twist of her head. "The new man?"

"He's here?"

Mary nodded. "He sure is. He's tall and handsome. *Very* handsome. But he's closer to your age than mine."

Lori chuckled. This town lived for matchmaking opportunities. "Don't go there, Mary."

"Why not? I've just been reading an article on how hot office romances are."

Lori picked up her briefcase and purse again. "Not for me they aren't. When I'm at the office, I work."

"Oh, I know that. You work very hard. But you might take a second look at Sean Matheson."

Lori made a face. "I doubt if I'll have a choice."

"Let me know what you think of him though."

"All right, I will. See you later, Mary."

The small hallway behind the reception office led into a space that had once been two rooms. Now it was partitioned with removable gray canvas dividers to make four offices: one for Lori; one for each of the full-time architectural technicians, Bob Bryan and Alan Smith; one for an occasional part-time worker.

Lori entered her small work space. Ignoring the clutter—rolled drawings stacked in the corner, diskettes stuffed into plastic storage boxes, and an overflowing file basket—she hung her coat on the wooden hanger dangling over the edge of one wall. She turned on her computer and listened to the chimes. At the same time, her phone buzzed.

"It's Ken, Lori. Do you want to come into my office and meet Sean Matheson?"

Mary had probably alerted Ken of her arrival. "Right away," Lori said.

She took her purse to the powder room and brushed the wind tangles from her hair, put a little more liner around her blue eyes, and smoothed the creases in her navy jacket and pants. The chunky heels on her soft black leather boots gave her the added height she liked when doing business with men.

That's your main problem, you resent that he's a man.

Maybe Susan was right.

Lori returned to her office, stored her purse away and straightened her shoulders. *Well, here goes.*

Ken's office was located in the former living room of the house. Peter's office was next door in what had been the dining room. She rarely saw Peter in the winter; he lived in the country, a long commute from the office, and often didn't make it in. Even though Peter brought in the majority of large jobs, Lori had never worked with him. It was Ken who dealt with the staff; Peter stayed aloof from the employees.

Ken's door was ajar. Lori rapped her knuckles against a panel and glanced around the corner.

Ken rose from his chair when he saw her. "Come on in, Lori."

A man who had been sitting in one of the maroon leather armchairs also stood up. He was easily six foot, with wavy, pale brown hair framing lean features. His black suit, perfectly fitting his broad shoulders and narrow hips, appeared formal next to Ken's gray slacks, blue shirt, and colorful golf tee tie.

When Ken introduced them, Sean's brilliant green gaze rested on her face. "I'm very pleased to meet you, Lori." His warm fingers folded into hers.

Mary was right: He was attractive. Lori tried to minimize her reaction to him by shaking his hand briefly. "I'm pleased to meet you as well."

Ken moved to his door and pulled it fully open. "Lori, Sean's going to have the space beside the main office. Introduce him to the rest of the staff and make sure he has everything he needs. As we've discussed, Sean, Lori has been working on the preliminary design for the job. She'll take you up to the lodge to meet George Hinton and you can all get the ball rolling."

"Thank you, Ken." Sean shook Ken's hand and grabbed his black wool overcoat that was slung over a chair. Tucking the coat over his arm, he indicated for Lori to move out into the carpeted corridor in front of him.

They walked down the narrow hallway, side by side, Sean's arm occasionally brushing hers.

"Rotten weather," he said.

"Oh, it's quite usual in this area."

"I gathered that, being a ski area."

She heard the sarcasm. He might be easy on the eyes, but he obviously knew it. He was far too handsome, far too sure of himself, far too . . . *male.*

They reached the main office. She glanced impersonally at Sean. "Have you met Alan Smith and Bob Bryan yet?"

"Not yet," Sean said.

Lori noticed that Alan and Bob seemed to be reacting to Sean the same way she was—cautiously.

Alan, good-looking himself, shook his hand. Bob, plumper and more jovial, laughed awkwardly as he met Sean.

Lori then led the way to Sean's office. She pushed open the door of the office Ken had obviously been keeping for Sean Matheson. It was usually filled with computer parts and a telephone that was used for personal phone calls. Now a computer had been set up on the desk for Sean. Everything else, all the junk, had been cleared out. Probably Mark, Ken's teenage son, had been in over the weekend; Ken used Mark for his computer expertise.

Sean tossed his overcoat on a chair and loosened his tie. He glanced at the computer. "Are your computers networked?"

"Not yet. Ken has very reluctantly joined the electronic age."

"I figured that out from what he said." Sean unbuttoned his suit jacket and hung it over the back of the desk chair. "He was very adamant that I be computer literate."

"Probably because most clients are asking for their drawings to be computer generated now."

"That's true." He smiled at her.

His smile was quite dazzling. Lori said quickly, "Obviously we're going to be working on Hinton's together, so why don't I go and get you the files? I'll also give you a couple of diskettes and some drawings. You can see how the job is progressing."

"That would be great, Lori. Thank you."

Relieved to leave him for a moment, Lori escaped to her office. She knelt down in front of her two-drawer filing cabinet. Her hands fumbled the files, and she gritted her teeth. She knew she was foolish to get too upset about Sean, but she couldn't stop the emotions trampling inside her.

After she found all the files, she rifled through her diskettes and pulled two. She rolled a couple of sketches and slipped a rubber band around them. That would keep him busy for a day or two.

Lori returned to Sean's office and put everything down on his desk. Sean, in shirtsleeves now, was sitting at his new desk looking through the drawers.

"Mary will help you with your supplies," Lori told him, wishing she wasn't quite so conscientious and could let him fend for himself and flounder around . . . even though she was sure he wasn't the type of man to flounder. She also wished he wasn't so attractive. Why couldn't he have been skinny under his suit jacket, instead of having broad shoulders that filled out his white shirt?

He closed a drawer. "I'll check out what I need."

To stop her hands from trembling, Lori thrust them deep into her jacket pockets. But she couldn't eliminate the tremor in her voice. "All you have to do is turn on the computer. You don't need a password. I'll make the appointment to see George tomorrow. The roads up to the lodge will be bad today."

Sean didn't seem to notice she was agitated. He reached out for the files and she saw an expensive gold watch encircling his strong masculine wrist. The elegance of the overcoat, the suit, the silk tie, and the watch made her wonder why he would leave a Manhattan firm for a small town one, where most of the time the men dressed in khakis and casual shirts. She wondered, too, if he was taking a drastic drop in salary.

"Thank you, Lori," he said. "It will take me a few days to settle in."

Lori moved her gaze to his face. He *was* good-looking . . . *very* good-looking . . . *extremely* good-looking . . . but she wouldn't be bowled over by him like Mary. *No way.* She cleared her throat. "Fine. Then I'll leave you to it." She walked to the door. "If you need me, you can just ring extension six on the phone."

He glanced at his phone, then at Lori. "What extension am I?"

"Oh, I think you're four in here."

"No one ever use this office?"

"Yes. Once. Ken had an associate when I first came here. Jed retired."

Sean leaned back in the tilting chair. He stretched out his long legs. "Ken mentioned you worked here during summer vacations from college."

Did he have to sprawl in front of her so casually? Lori crunched her fingers into her palms and felt her nails bite her flesh. She exhaled a breath. What else had Ken told Sean about her? Ken was sort of enigmatic. She never really knew what he thought about her work. She presumed, because he had hired her to work here, that he thought she was a good architect and a complement to the firm.

Sean was waiting for her to speak.

She had to clear her throat again. "Yes, I did. But then, this is the only architectural practice in town."

"True. They are few and far between in this area." Sean placed his hands on the padded arms of the chair.

Lori saw his fingers grip the arms, making her realize he wasn't very relaxed either. A silence, taut with tension, hung between them.

What was it about him? She could talk to Alan or Bob all day and not have her heart feel as if it were a hard lump threatening to rise and choke her.

Sean's brilliant gaze focused on her. "All right?"

No. She wasn't all right. She was feeling very unsteady on her legs and extremely strange—sort of light-headed. She had to get out of here. "I'll see you later," she told him and quickly left his office.

The hallway seemed to contain much cooler air than the air in his office. Once out of the range, Lori leaned against the wall for a moment. Her reaction was silly and likely had nothing to do with Sean. She had probably gotten herself so worked up over the weekend, she was feeling the weakening effects of all that expended indignation.

Lori returned to her desk and began to fiddle on her computer. She found herself absently playing a game of Solitaire. She shouldn't be wasting her time; she had tons of work to do. She closed down the game. But instead of opening the file containing her drawing, she rested her chin on her palm and stared out the window at the falling snow. She needed a cup of coffee. She picked up her mug, which read, "I'm the boss," on the side, and walked to the kitchen.

Sean was in the kitchen waiting for the coffee to finish brewing. He stood with his lean hips resting on the edge of the counter, leafing through a glossy architectural magazine.

He briefly looked in her direction and folded the magazine. "Hi. How are you doing?"

"Working hard," she fibbed, avoiding looking at him. But she was extremely aware of him as she wandered over to a bulletin board tacked with messages. She read the notices she had already read before, swinging her mug from her fingers.

"Lori, the coffee's ready."

She turned around. Sean had put down the magazine and was holding the glass carafe, expecting to pour her drink first. Hurriedly she put her mug down on the countertop and he poured her coffee. He was being polite—she realized that—but she would prefer to be treated as one of the boys. She was quite capable of doing everything herself.

"Do you take any cream or sugar, or do you like a full cup of black?"

"A full cup of black, please."

He finished pouring but before she could pick up her mug, he twisted it around and read the words on it. He smiled. "Is this the truth? Are you the real boss around here?"

"No. It's just a joke. The guys in the office bought it for me last Christmas." She picked up the mug and cupped it between her hands.

Sean served his own coffee in one of the white cups and saucers they used for guests. "Maybe they had a reason."

His tone suggested he was challenging her. She shrugged her shoulders. "You'll find out, won't you?"

"Will I?"

Pulsing tension beat between them once more. She could feel herself grow breathless. "Ken and Peter are the bosses around here."

Sean raised an eyebrow. "Until Ken retires, that is."

"Ken's not retiring."

"Oh? He mentioned to me that he might consider slowing down over the next few years."

Lori knew the shock must be evident in her expression. Ken had never told her he might retire or slow down. "Ken actually told you that?"

Sean sipped some coffee. "Yes, when he came to New York to interview me. I wanted to get into a firm where I had some chance for advancement."

"You mean, you would like to become a partner?"

"Absolutely."

Lori couldn't believe what she was hearing. She had dreaded Sean's arrival, mainly because she liked being the third architect in the practice. And her status *did* make her Bob and Alan's boss to some degree. She certainly hadn't thought of Ken taking on a man to be groomed as his possible replacement. Matheson & Rhodes, or Rhodes & Matheson?

"Aren't you looking for promotional possibilities as well?" Sean asked.

"Well, of course. But my plans are a little different. I'm not staying here. I'm going into my own business." She had already figured out that she would never make partner with two men like Ken and Peter. Alone would be the only way she would achieve her aim of being Ashton Heights' first woman architect.

Sean raised an eyebrow. "Soon?"

"Not right away, but in a couple of years."

"You don't see any possibility of advancement here?"

She didn't want to mention that Ken and Peter were members of an established boy's club to which she would never gain entrance. Men didn't seem to understand those things. They didn't see the barriers. Her father couldn't comprehend her fighting attitude at times, though her mother and sister understood. She also didn't want Sean to think she felt any way but positive. She said brightly. "I think there's a good chance for advancement here, but I want to be on my own."

He sipped his coffee. "I understand why you would want to be your own boss. My sister is a lawyer. She's always said she has to work harder than men to prove herself. She has her own law firm now and is happier for being on her own."

Lori hadn't expected Sean's empathy. She didn't want him to recognize her struggle. She would rather keep him in the position of interloper; it was safer. If he were on her level, she might discover his attraction was more than aesthetic.

"She's probably right," she admitted.

"I know she's right, and I suspect you have a similar situation on your hands."

Lori gave him a narrow look. What was his game? Had he detected her antagonism? Was this some type of ploy to win her over? "I don't have a *situation*. I'm merely here for a couple of years to gain experience before I start my own company. I'm an independent type. I really don't like working for other people." She gave him what she hoped was a cool businesslike smile and walked to the door. "Now, I must get back to work. See you later."

Lori walked too fast away from the kitchen. The coffee in her mug swilled and hot liquid spilled over her hand. She sat down at her desk and wiped the drips off her hand and mug with a tissue. She sipped some coffee, and looked at the screensaver she had made for herself of an ambitious domed building. Did she really think she would have the chance to ever build anything like that? Reality was that, even with her own business, she would be a slave to the desires of wealthy clients.

She didn't want Sean to see the design, which was entirely unpractical, so she quickly clicked her properties section with the mouse and replaced her customized screensaver with one of the standard ones. Then she opened her drawing and pored over a list of changes she had to make. But it took a great deal of effort to force herself to concentrate on the job at hand and not even think about Sean Matheson.

When she needed a break, Lori called George Hinton's office. George was a self-made millionaire who owned two big ski resorts just outside of town, and was now developing a third. When Ken had handed Lori the job, she had been thrilled. She had never been on top of a project this big, and she saw it as a chance to expose her architectural prowess—to prove her design capabilities. But now she had someone else alongside of her, who possibly had his own ideas and would limit her own talent.

"I'm bringing another architect with me," she told George.

"Ken did say there was someone new coming into the firm," George said in his gruff voice. "I was wondering if he was going to put him on my job."

"Well, he has." She tried not to sound as if Sean's

intervention mattered to her. "When do you want to meet with us?"

They set up a meeting for the next morning at ten o'clock, and Lori called through to Sean's office to tell him.

"Thanks, Lori. Hey, what do you do for lunch around here?"

Lori glanced out of the window. It was still snowing. "If the weather is really bad we sometimes call out for pizza, or there's a restaurant down the road with a menu that has everything on it. Or you can bring your own lunch. There's a microwave and a toaster oven in the kitchen."

"I didn't bring my lunch. Why don't we go out to the restaurant that has everything? It will give us time to chat about the job."

Lori knew she didn't have much choice. She had to eat lunch anyway, and they would have to discuss the job sooner or later. *Get it over with.* "I'll meet you at the door at one," she said. "I always go at one."

"One is fine for me. I've got a four-wheel-drive sports utility wagon, so we don't have to worry about the snow."

Good for you, she thought as she hung up the phone. She had lived in a ski resort area all her life and she only drove an ordinary car with perfectly ordinary all-weather tires—not even snow tires. Probably, because he had lived in Manhattan, he presumed everyone here in the country drove sports utility vehicles.

For the next hour Lori really couldn't settle down to work. She didn't know quite what she was feeling. She was sure she wasn't attracted to Sean, however handsome he was. He was merely one of those men women took a second look at. What she was experiencing was normal trepidation about going out to lunch with another architect—a new architect she had to work with. *Oh, Ken why did you do this to me? I would have been perfectly content here for another two years. I had my life designed.*

While Mary was at lunch, Jennifer Stanley, the accountant, worked the reception desk. Jennifer's plump smiling face, short blonde curls, and casual slacks and sweater changed the atmosphere of the outer office. She had the desk strewn with a paperback book, a sandwich, and a crossword puzzle.

Lori pulled on her gloves while waiting by the main door for Sean.

"Venturing out in this icky weather?" Jennifer asked during a lull in the phone calls.

Lori nodded. "I'm going out to lunch with Sean."

"Wow. Isn't he *gorgeous?*"

"When did you meet him?" Jennifer didn't come into the office until ten o'clock each day so Lori hadn't been able to introduce her to Sean.

"He came by my office looking for the kitchen, and popped his head in and said, 'Here's someone I haven't met yet,' so we introduced ourselves and I told him I was responsible for payroll, so be nice to me."

Lori smiled, but didn't remark because Sean came into the reception area, shrugging into his black overcoat.

"Ready?" he asked and added a smile for Jennifer. "Hi."

"Hi, Sean," Jennifer said flirtatiously. "Have a nice lunch and drive carefully."

"Will do," Sean told her, seeing Lori through the door.

They stood on the steps, pulled their collars up around their necks, then dashed across the icy parking lot to Sean's dark green four-wheel drive. He opened the passenger door and ushered Lori in, then hopped in himself and started the engine. While he climbed out and brushed away the snow from the windshield and rear window, Lori sat and shivered until the heater warmed up.

When he returned, he said, "You can direct me to the restaurant." He glanced over his shoulder to back out of the parking space.

"It's not far. You just go out of here and turn right. Two lights down on your right. It's called The Heights."

Sean seemed larger inside the vehicle than he did in the office, and Lori shrank back into her seat. She felt very awkward with him and tried to distract herself by looking around. Some maps were pushed down between the front seats, but the rest of the interior seemed tidy. Which probably made sense because there was still a new smell to the dark gray upholstery.

Sean glanced at her. "Problems?"

"No. Not at all." She feigned cheerfulness. "Where are you staying?"

"The Winds Hotel. You probably know it. It's out on the highway. A nice place, but very crowded this time of year." He smiled at her. "I had to fight ski poles all the way to the door this morning."

Desperate to be casual with him, Lori chuckled. "That's how most of the hotels around here make their money." The Winds was a high class establishment, with pools, saunas, and fancy restaurants. She wondered if the company was footing his hotel bill.

The Heights was a huge A-frame wooden building. Brass lanterns attached to the stone walls cast a warm yellow glow over the dark wooden booths, and tables and chairs. They chose a booth in a corner near the back window that overlooked some small ski slopes. A log fire burned in the stone grate. Lori thought that everything around here had a sort of *apres-ski* atmosphere lately.

Sean hung their coats on a hook by the booth, and they sat down. Lori noticed the contrast in hue between Sean's throat and the collar of his white shirt. The low light accentuated the lean angles of Sean's handsome features. He definitely had a tropical glow on his skin.

"Have you been away on vacation?" she asked.

He rearranged the cutlery on the paper place mat so that it was symmetrical. "I had a week in the Bahamas before I came here."

"Smart move considering the weather." Lori wondered if he had gone alone or with a woman. She didn't ask. He might even be married for all she knew, although he didn't wear a wedding ring.

His gaze settled on her face. "Have you been to the Bahamas, Lori?"

Did he think she looked winter pale? "No, I haven't. Bermuda is as far south as I've been."

"I've been to Bermuda as well, but I thought the Bahamas were great. I recommend it."

The waitress came over to their table. They both ordered the soup and sandwich special. During their meal Lori discovered that Sean must have read the files quite thoroughly, because he asked pertinent questions to the Hinton job. There was no more talk of the Bahamas, or why he had re-located to be a small town architect, or anything personal about him. And he only took the designated hour. By ten to two they were on their way back to the office.

"A beneficial working lunch," Sean said as he parked next to Ken's Mercedes.

"I hope I've been helpful," Lori told him, and climbed out of the wagon. She didn't feel comfortable with him, and she was sure she was going to have a hard time working with him.

Mary was back now. She smiled at them. "Stopped snowing?"

"It stopped while we were having lunch, Mary," Sean said and went through to his office.

Lori didn't manage to slip by Mary so easily.

"How was lunch with Sean?"

"All business," Lori said.

"Don't you think he's handsome?" Mary asked softly.

"I suppose, if you like that lean-featured type." Lori went to collect her phone messages. She noticed a basket had now been allotted to Sean. At the moment it was empty, but it would soon fill up as he became known as a part of the firm.

"So you're not attracted?" Mary went on.

Lori shook her head firmly. "No. Not at all."

Mary shrugged. "Too bad, because I've discovered he's single and unattached."

As she walked to her office, Lori thought that was the *last* thing she wanted to know about Sean.

Chapter Two

Lori spent the entire afternoon with Ken and Sean, huddled over the table in the boardroom adjoining Ken's office. At the finish, Lori was loaded with changes that had to be made to her plans before the next morning's meeting. She took home a roll of drawings and a briefcase full of files and diskettes.

Because the snow had stopped, the roads were clear. Her driveway had already been plowed by the condominium maintenance contractor, so she drove her car straight in to the garage to park.

Her house was a narrow three-story home in a picturesque housing development designed by Randall & Rhodes and built by her father. She had purchased a unit last year and didn't regret moving from her parents' house. She often took work home, and living with her parents wasn't conducive to it. Her mother was employed by an animal shelter, and when the shelter ran out of space, the cats came home with her. There were cats crawling around all over the house. Her father worked crazy hours and was always renovating the home. When her older sister, Julie, finally left to try and find fame and fortune in the California music scene, Lori decided to leave the chaos, too. Now she had her own minimalist decor and her life in at least partial order.

She unloaded all her work on to the tiled floor in her hallway, stripped off her coat and boots, and ran her fingers through her tousled hair. It felt good to be home.

The phone rang and Lori winced. Away from the office, ringing phones grated on her nerves. She nearly left the call to the answering machine, but decided to grab the phone in the kitchen. It was her mother.

"How are you feeling today?" Alice asked.

"I met him."

"And?"

"He's okay, I suppose."

"But you're still upset about him?"

"Yes."

"Oh, dear. Well, you know these things do happen in life."

"So I've been told all weekend." Lori didn't want to discuss Sean anymore. "So what's going on in the real world?"

"Julie's coming back from L.A. next week."

"For good?" Julie had cut a CD, but nothing had happened for her yet.

"I'm not sure if it's for good, but it's for a while. She's recording another CD in New York City soon."

"Well, that's great she's coming home." Lori always missed her sister, more than she would admit.

"It is. There's only one problem."

Lori felt her stomach sink. More problems she didn't need. "What?"

"Your father has decided to build on to the side of the house where your bedrooms were."

"Our bedrooms *were?*"

"They'll be back, but larger. However, while he's putting on another extension, Lori, there is no room for Julie. And since you have three bedrooms, she was wondering. . . ."

Oh no. "Mom."

"It's only for a couple of weeks or so, until she goes to New York."

"I suppose," Lori said, knowing she sounded less than enthusiastic about having Julie stay with her. She loved her sister, but she couldn't cope with visitors while she was working.

Alice laughed. "You girls will have fun together."

"I'm working, Mom."

"So is Julie. She says she has to write some songs."

Well, maybe that wouldn't be so bad. "In that case, what can I say?"

"Not 'no' to your own family, that's for sure. Thanks, Sweetie. She's coming home next Tuesday. Now, one other thing."

Lori raised her eyes to her kitchen ceiling. "Yes?"

"Do you want a cat? I've got the sweetest little black and—"

"Mom. *That* I *can* say 'no' to. I like living alone in perfect peace. Doesn't anyone understand that?"

"I sure don't."

"I know. You're not happy unless Dad is playing with power tools and knocking down walls."

"Well, it does get a little much sometimes, but he's made such a great big house out of this little bungalow."

Lori couldn't dispute that. An entire second floor had been added at one time. Lori had designed the new sun room Jack Fenton had built on last summer.

"Will you be over to visit on the weekend?" her mother asked.

"Yes. I'll drop over on Sunday."

"What are you doing Saturday? Don't tell me you have a date?"

"No. I'm probably working."

"You work far too hard, Lori. You should be thinking about getting married and having a baby . . ."

"Mom, no. I want to have my own architectural firm first."

"You might be too old for children by then."

"No, I won't. I'm planning to go out on my own in two years."

"But it'll take a while to work up your business."

"I know. But it's the gamble I have to take."

"You are taking a gamble, Sweetie—with time."

"Mom. Look at my friend, Penny. She quit college and rushed into marriage. Within two years Doug had walked out on her and now she's really struggling with the baby. All she's got is a job at a supermarket."

"Doug was a no-good lout from the beginning."

"That's not the point. If she had finished college, she could have a better job and be able to support herself and a child. It makes sense."

"Lori, there are a lot of college grads without good jobs. It just depends on what happens."

"That's another point, Mom. I'm not going to let my life depend on what happens. I'm going to make everything go my way. I want to be in control."

"Well, I wish you luck. I just wonder what would happen if you did fall in love."

She immediately thought of Sean. But she said firmly, "Nothing would happen."

"But love is urgent."

"Mom, if a man loved me, he would wait, wouldn't he?"

"I suppose," her mother said dubiously. "I do have an aunt whose husband made her wait until he finished his education."

"There you are. Men have done it. Men make *women* wait."

"Some men. Your father certainly didn't want to wait. He was most eager to get married."

"And that's fine, Mom. Different strokes and all that. Anyway, this is all hypothetical. In reality, I'm not in love and I have a ton of work to do for a meeting tomorrow morning."

"Then I'll let you go. Take care and don't get too uptight about that new guy. See you on Sunday."

Lori hung up the phone and sighed. If anyone could make her doubt her convictions, it was her mother. She did want a family, but in the future, not right now, this very minute.

The phone rang again. She picked it up.

"It's Sue, Lori. How did it go?"

"I survived."

"Is your *man* problem a hunk?"

Lori had to be truthful. "Let's say he's aesthetically pleasing."

Susan chuckled. "An architectural term, I presume, for saying he's super cool."

"He's good-looking. Leave it at that."

"Are you . . ."

"Sue. I'm not attracted to him, and I've no intention of being."

"Well, I just thought that if you were, it might soothe your soul. You were so upset over the weekend."

"I'm still upset about losing full control over my job. And, to cap it off, apparently he's being groomed to be a partner."

"Ouch," Susan said. "Do you want me to come over?"

"No, it's okay. I've got to work. Thanks, anyway."

"Oh, well. If you need me, call."

"I will. Thanks, Susie."

"Talk to you later, Lori. Don't work too hard."

Easier said than done, Lori decided as she cooked her dinner before going upstairs to begin work. She knew the changes would take her most of the night.

When the alarm buzzed in the morning, Lori reached out and turned it off so she could sleep longer. She awoke again to bright sunshine, and realized that she would have to really hurry to reach the office on time. She rushed as much as she could but Sean's wagon was already parked when she arrived.

Lori trudged through the snow-plowed parking lot, thinking that he must be the efficient type.

Mary said, "Morning, Lori. He's asking for you."

Lori juggled her briefcase and a roll of drawings. "He?"

"Sean. He said you have a meeting up at Hinton's this morning."

"Not until ten o'clock for heaven's sake."

"Oh. I was under the impression it was earlier. He was here before me. Ken must have given him a key."

At least she also had a key. Sean wasn't privileged in that regard. "I'll go and see him."

Lori walked through the office. She dumped her things on her desk, took off her coat, and went to Sean's office. He was sitting at his desk reading some correspondence from the Hinton files, more casually dressed today in gray slacks, a maroon shirt, black tie, and a gray v-neck sweater. The dark colors made his hair appear lighter and his features very handsome.

"Good morning," she said.

He looked up. "Good morning, Lori."

"Mary said you were anxious to speak to me."

"I just wanted to know how long it took to get to the ski resort."

"About twenty minutes."

"That's fine then."

"You didn't think I was going to make it, did you?"

He rested his hands on the file, moving his pen between his fingers. "Did *you?*"

Lori pushed aside a strand of stray hair. "No. I turned off the first alarm."

"What don't you like: early mornings, cold winter mornings, or meetings?"

"All of the above."

He chuckled. "I'm using the hotel telephone service to wake me up at the moment."

"You have a hard time as well?" Judging by the neat way he dressed, the tidy state of his car, and the way he had kept within the hour for lunch yesterday, she didn't think he would have faults, or not visible ones anyway.

"Yes. I've tried going to bed earlier, but it doesn't help. I've come to the conclusion I just like to sleep."

"I know I go to bed too late," Lori told him, realizing that they were having an extremely personal conversation. Sean certainly seemed more human this morning. Too human. She saw that his jaw had been freshly shaved and she could smell a crisp aftershave that made her think of sharp mountain air.

He seemed to be watching her reaction to him and Lori shifted her feet around on the carpet. "I had better go and get ready for the meeting."

"I'll come by your office. We'll allow ourselves half an hour to get there."

"Fine."

She dashed back to her office and sat down at her computer, feeling quite warm in her red sweater and black slacks. She wore them because she knew they would probably go out on the construction site.

Sean came by a while later. Over his clothes he had put on a quilted black leather bomber jacket. His brown hair had gold streaks which she hadn't noticed yesterday. He tapped a pair of black leather gloves on his palm. "Lori, are you ready to go?"

She rolled the prints of the new drawings Bob had plotted for her. Then she put on her coat and picked up her black leather purse. "Yes, I'm ready. Do you have the other drawings?"

"I put them in my wagon already."

She felt annoyed that he hadn't even considered taking her car. "Right."

He glanced at her but said nothing as they left the office building and walked across the parking lot.

"Can you tell me how to get there?" Sean asked as they drove out on to the road.

Lori explained they had to drive through town and out about half a mile on the highway. "The Ski Lodge is well marked on a sign."

"Thanks."

She couldn't stand it any longer. The pressure inside had built to bursting point. She had to say something to him. "We could have taken my car."

"It's fine," he said, with a brief smile.

"Don't you like riding with women?" She knew she sounded confrontational.

He stopped for a red light at the intersection of a spired stone church and a gas station. "Lori, what does it matter?"

She glanced out of the window, which was quickly becoming encrusted with the sloppy slush from the road. "I guess it doesn't matter." But it *did* matter— not because it mattered whose vehicle they traveled in, but because it all related to Sean coming in and taking over.

"I don't have a problem with you. All right?"

He sounded so stern that Lori winced. She had made

him angry. She hadn't meant to do that. She had meant
to keep their working relationship businesslike.

"*Also*, you think I've butted in on your domain,
don't you?"

Of course he'd guessed that as well. He was obviously very perceptive. Maybe because he had a sister.

She turned back to look at him and told the truth.
"I thought this job was mine alone."

"I don't know why. Judging by the amount of work
we have to do, I would say you wouldn't have been
able to handle the load by yourself." He sprayed the
windshield washer fluid and set the wipers in motion.

Lori stared through the streaked windshield. The
bright sun made the streaks even more visible. The
wipers kept moving.

"You obviously worked late into last night. You
can't keep that up, Lori."

"It's to be expected in a small firm."

"To some extent, yes. But I think Ken understands
you work long hours and now he's hired me to help
out. If we can't work together, then some other arrangements will have to be made."

Lori knew if she didn't behave more professionally
and treat him fairly, she was going to destroy the faith
that everyone had in her. Sean might complain to Ken
about her. Then her father would find out. She cleared
her throat. "I'm willing to see how it goes."

"That's one round won," Sean said.

Lori promised herself not to get caught in any more

conversations like this with Sean. She had given away all her apprehension and anxiety. She had made herself vulnerable. But not again.

Lori directed him up the steep hill to the ski resort. After climbing the hill they reached an intersection of roads with a number of quaint white sign posts.

"These are signs to an existing hotel and the ski slopes," she told Sean. "The new development will be on the other side of the hill. George's office is attached to his own home. He lives up here. If you take that narrow plowed road, you will eventually come to his house; you can park outside his office."

Sean turned up the narrow road. They were in a higher, cooler elevation, and the tires squeaked over the packed snow. "We'll go see the site afterwards," he said.

"All right." Lori smoothed her coat over her knees.

Sean parked beside the sign that read, "Office." He opened his door and climbed out. Lori jumped down to the snowy driveway. Sean went to the back of the wagon and took out the other roll of drawings and they walked up the pathway together. Lori could tell that Sean was still irritated with her because he held his body away from her. Not that she wanted him closer to her, but she preferred it when they were more friendly. Why hadn't she just accepted Ken's decision to put Sean on the Hinton job with her and not made a fuss? Why had she hinted at being uptight in her career because she was a woman? Why couldn't she just relax when she was with Sean?

As Sean opened the door to George's office and stood to one side to let her through, she forced herself to be gracious. From now on she was going to be extremely composed in Sean's presence and show him that she could work affably with him. There would be no more problems between them.

Lori had been surprised the first time she had met George Hinton. George had been born into an influential family who had owned half the town at one time, and he had capitalized on that wealth and created more. She had expected a large-framed man designed to fit the booming voice she had heard over the phone. Not the case. Today, he stood a slim five-foot-nine in jeans and a blue sweater with a skier knitted into the front. His salt-and-pepper hair receded from his broad forehead.

"Coats off," George told them briskly after the introductions. "We'll go into my boardroom."

George found hangers for their coats in the closet. There was no one in the front office today, though sometimes George's pretty blonde daughter, Elaine, came in to do office and accounting work.

"Elaine not in today?" Lori asked conversationally as they were shown to the oblong polished table in front of a big window. She could see one of the ski slopes with tiny figures dotting the hillside.

George shook his head. "She went to Portugal with

her mother to soak up the sun. I'll order coffee from the hotel today."

George left them for a moment and Sean unrolled the drawings, which were mostly of George's existing resorts. Included were a few hand sketches that Lori had drawn after the initial meetings. She unrolled her revised designs.

Sean glanced at them and then went to stand by the window, hands in his pockets. Lori wished he would speak to her and break the film of ice that was forming between them. Or maybe she should speak first.

"So what do you think?" she asked.

He turned around. "About what?"

"About George?"

"I've barely met him."

"True." She swallowed hard.

He glanced out of the window again.

George returned and Lori felt relieved that the stilted conversation didn't have to continue. A few moments later, coffee was delivered from the hotel in a silver pot with thick white cups and saucers set on a silver tray.

Everyone sat down around the table. George at one end, Sean in the middle on one side, Lori halfway up the other side. George poured coffee for everyone.

Sean conducted the meeting. He wanted to know exactly what George had in mind for the project.

Lori grew more agitated. What George had in mind for the project was well documented in the files, and in her initial sketches and recent designs. They had also gone over a lot in the meeting yesterday with Ken. Nonetheless, Sean made George go through everything again. Lori knew George didn't have much savvy about the actual drawing, but he knew what he wanted and could describe his needs quite adequately. Sean seemed to have no problem with the new hotel facility, but he questioned the extra accommodation units.

"You want these twenty five units built on this hillside?" Sean asked, pointing to the site plan.

"Yes. But Ken did say that might be a problem."

She had mentioned that problem, Lori thought, but she didn't say anything. Sean wasn't inviting her comments. He wasn't even looking at her.

"You wouldn't consider leveling the site?" Sean asked.

"No," George said firmly. "I want the units built on the hill, overlooking the slopes. Otherwise they won't have the view the hotel rooms have."

Lori knew that George also wanted the units to be two-story with spiral staircases. She did mention this.

"Okay." Sean used a mechanical pencil to indicate the detail on the plan. "Is this going to be an open loft area above the spirals?"

"It could be," George said. "However, I don't want to make the units too fancy. I want to keep costs low."

He wanted the fanciest chalets in the world, but he wanted them cheaply built. Sean obviously caught on and looked at Lori. They swapped exasperated glances, their personal feud momentarily forgotten.

George added. "My wife has her heart set on the spirals."

Lori stared up at the ceiling and vented her frustration on the pot lights. She wanted to keep calm.

They went over more details and new ideas that George had come up with, for both the hotel and the units. After a while it was obvious they would have to present completely new designs to incorporate the changes.

Sean said, "We'll need another meeting. What's a good time for you at the beginning of next week, George?"

"Tuesday morning, like today, is fine for me. Same time."

"Tuesday, same time then," Sean said, beginning to roll up the drawings.

Lori helped him, knowing she would be working the weekend to get the work done on time.

They retrieved their coats and Sean told George they were going to look at the site.

George looked at Sean. "I want you to get a good handle on this job, Sean."

"We'll deal with it," Sean reassured him and shook his hand.

Lori also shook George's hand. Then she walked outside into the crisp air. She drew in a couple of breaths and let them out. Her chest felt as tight as if she had been running a marathon since early Monday morning. *I want you to get a good handle on the job, Sean.*

They climbed into Sean's vehicle again. He drove around the corner and up another hill to the building site.

After he turned off the engine, Sean said, "Now, what's wrong?"

Lori was seething about George's comment. He had made it sound as if Lori hadn't been doing a good job, as if she hadn't had a *handle* on it. But she wasn't going to say anything to Sean about that. She needed to lighten up when she was with him. She cleared her throat and said, "Oh, George. He wants everything for nothing."

"Yes," Sean agreed. "We might have to cut down on something. We'll see. Are you available to come into the office on Saturday? It would give us a chance to work away from interruptions."

"I'm in most Saturdays," she said.

"Okay. Great." He picked up his gloves and put them on. "So let's go look at this site."

Lori slipped out of the door on to the gravel pathway.

Sean joined her and put on sunglasses.

Lori brushed back a strand of hair that had blown out of place and her arm touched Sean's. She felt him move away from her. She fished her own dark glasses from her purse and put them on. She would survive this, but she wasn't going to act any way but professional from now on.

Lori pointed as they walked. "The new lodge is going into that valley and the chalets will be built on that hillside. Then George is going to put in some new chairlifts that will go up to the slopes from here. He's going to develop some more ambitious slopes on this side."

"Looks good, except for building those units down this hillside. It's very steep."

"We're going to have to compromise on that."

"You think he'll compromise?"

"I'm not sure. He hasn't given in yet. Ken's attitude, when we met the last time, was build them and hope there's a landslide."

Sean's laughter was harsh. "Nice to think, but we can't do that."

"Of course not. Ken was only joking."

"I know that."

Lori bit back a retort and turned to walk to the road. Sean moved beside her, rubbing his hands. "It's freezing out here. Let's go for some lunch."

They stopped for grilled cheese sandwiches at a small diner. The same as at lunch yesterday, they only discussed the job. Then Sean drove back to the office.

Lori spent the afternoon worrying. She had made some mistakes today. She hoped Sean wouldn't tell tales to Ken. She made up her mind that from now on, she had to watch herself in every way with Sean.

Just after five o'clock she saw Sean's vehicle leave. Then Alan and Bob left. She supposed she should go home. She shut off her computer and began to close down her office. Ken came by as she was slipping some items into her briefcase, and her stomach sank. There was only one reason Ken would come by to see her; Sean had blabbed.

Ken slouched in her other chair. "So how's it going?"

"Busy," she said, tossing more items into her briefcase. Her throat ached with tension. Why hadn't she controlled her words and actions with Sean?

"I suppose I really mean, how's it going with Sean?"

She moistened her lips and smiled at Ken. "Fine."

"Lori, you're being quite obtuse. Aren't you getting along with Sean?"

"Yes, of course I am. Has he told you differently?"

"No. He's not said a word to me about you."

Relief made her giddy. "Then what's the problem?"

"You. I suspect you didn't like it that I've put him on the Hinton job. But, whatever you think, you couldn't handle a project of that size by yourself. Sean's a good man. He's worked on some large buildings in Manhattan. He won a student award for design in his last year of college. I think he'll be perfect. And it will also give you a chance to learn teamwork."

Lori sat down in her chair opposite Ken. This discussion was getting serious. "Are you saying I'm not very good at working on a team?"

"You like full control, don't you?"

"Yes, I do. But I worked on team projects in college."

He smiled. "I know; and you came through with high marks. But this is different. The clients are real, clients who aren't easy to get along with, clients who give us unreasonable demands and deadlines. I do think you'll find that Sean is good to work with. Really, I do."

Lori nodded. She didn't want to cause dissension because she had personal aspirations that weren't being met. "I think he'll work out as well."

"At least try. If you have any questions, come to me. All right?"

She agreed she would, but she knew she wouldn't. She was the type of person to try and work out all her dilemmas without help.

"Anyway," Ken said. "On a fun note, I thought I would have a get-together next Saturday evening. A week Saturday, not this weekend. Something for the staff. It would be a nice way to greet Sean into the firm. Caroline's willing to have a buffet dinner."

Lori didn't mean it as she said, "Sounds good." She didn't want to socialize with Sean any more than she had to. The occasional lunch was tolerable, but she'd rather avoid parties. Unfortunately, Ken's parties were unavoidable; He expected all the staff to show up and support him. And if she didn't attend, he would really think there were problems with Sean.

"Then you are free next weekend?"

"Yes. I'm free."

"Great. It'll be a chance to beat back the February blahs."

The February blahs, she thought, as she drove home. She definitely had them at this time of year. She wouldn't mind lazing on a warm beach, reading a book. Sean was smart. He had grabbed some time in the Bahamas before he came to the new job.

She turned into her driveway and pressed her remote for the garage. Why did she keep thinking about Sean? He seemed linked to her every thought.

Lori cooked herself a microwaved meal, and carried the tray up one level to her dining room overlooking her small, snow-logged yard. Instead of depressing herself with snow and darkness, she turned on the television and watched a silly sitcom while she ate. Afterwards, she went up another level to her office, sat down at her computer, and began to incorporate some of George's changes into the initial designs for the ski lodge. She was used to working each evening, then going to bed around ten o'clock, but tonight she couldn't seem to concentrate. Her mind kept wandering to Sean.

Eventually, she closed down, took a hot bath and went to bed.

Chapter Three

The early night must have helped, because Lori actually woke up on time and arrived at the office well before eight-thirty. Sean's vehicle was already there. Alan and Bob, who both came in well before eight, stopped her on her way to the kitchen.

"How's it going with Sean?" Alan asked.

She shrugged her shoulders. "It's going okay, I guess."

"If you dress like that every day we won't know who's who," Bob commented.

Lori had tucked her hair back into a clip with only a few wisps to soften the style beside her cheeks. Her black pantsuit was of a masculine style with a white silk shirt. "I want to look businesslike."

"Because of Sean?" Alan asked.

"I suppose." She sighed. "I feel like I have to keep on my toes."

"Maybe he's too 'big city' for you," Bob suggested.

"Possibly. He seems out of place here somehow. We all drive regular cars, but he has to have a four-wheel-drive *sports* vehicle, for heaven's sake as if that's what you need when you live here. It's like an image thing. I wouldn't be surprised if his shoes weren't . . ."

"Gucci?" A voice spoke softly behind her.

Her skin flushed, and Lori turned around to see Sean. Today he wore a pair of casual navy slacks and a navy sweater over a pale blue shirt and a darker tie. Why did he always look so well-groomed and so . . . handsome. "I wasn't . . ." she began.

"Yes. You were." Sean plunged his hands into his pockets. "I didn't buy the *sports* vehicle because I was moving here, Lori. I already owned it because I lived upstate from Manhattan. And my shoes are no-name, if you must know, with serviceable rubber soles for this changeable climate."

Sean turned around with an intentional squeak of those rubber soles, and walked back into his office.

Lori smiled sheepishly at the other two men. "Well, I put my foot in it."

"Or into his shoes at least," Alan said with a smirk.

"Definitely." Lori agreed. "Oh, well, I'll deal with him."

She walked into her corner, sat down at her desk,

and rubbed her forehead hard with her fingers. What had she done? Her big mouth had got her into trouble again. She had to apologize to Sean right away.

Drawing in a deep breath, Lori rose to her feet and went along to Sean's office. She knocked on the door and when there was no answer, she tentatively opened the door. She stared at his empty desk for a while before she realized he wasn't there. She exhaled her relief; this was a respite. However, she would still have to see him.

Lori noticed that Sean was settling in: he had filled some of the empty shelves with reference books, and there was a yellow pad of paper, pens, and a pile of files on the desk. She sat down in his chair, pulled the yellow pad before her and wrote, *Sean, I need to talk to you. Lori.*

With the ball now in his court, Lori returned to her desk. She tried to concentrate on her work, but she kept looking up each time she heard footsteps. Alan told her the coffee was ready.

"Thanks," she said.

"Talked to him yet?"

She shook her head.

"He went out."

"Probably gone to look for another job," she said wearily.

Alan smiled. "Ah, he'll understand. If not, then he doesn't have a sense of humor."

Lori hoped Alan was right. She worked for a little

longer, then went to the kitchen to fill her mug with fresh coffee. When she came back Sean was sitting in her other chair.

"Hi," he said. "You left me a note. You wanted to see me."

She sat down and fussed around finding a coaster for her mug. "Yes, I did." She knew this wasn't going to be easy. Sean's lean jaw appeared as if it were jumping with nerves.

She swallowed hard and plunged in. "I wanted to say I was sorry for what I said behind your back this morning. It was unwarranted, and—"

"Unprofessional?"

She nodded, mortified that he should come up with such a term for her, but it was the truth. She had acted unprofessionally with him from the start.

Sean shifted his shoulders as if he wanted to release some tension. "You're entitled to your opinion, Lori."

"I know, but—"

"Forget it, Lori. It's okay."

"Are you sure?" She didn't think he sounded as if he forgave her. In fact, she thought he sounded hurt.

"Yes. I'm sure." His smile was slight. "Let's forget the personal and concentrate on work."

"Yes, of course." She felt strictly put in her place.

She expected him to leave, but instead Sean hooked an arm over the chair back. "I do understand how you feel, Lori. Really, I do. But it's irrelevant to the situation as it stands now. I'm here. I'm staying. End of subject. So, are you ready to look at Hinton's in more detail?"

Work was really the only ground she felt safe on with him. She nodded quickly. "I made those changes to the designs last night."

"Then let's see them." He glanced around at her small space. "We'll meet in my office. We can spread out on the drawing board."

My office. But she stopped her thought from escalating. She wished her office were larger so that she didn't appear to be a position below him, but it wasn't. She wasn't going to let her agitation show. She had to get into step with Sean, not antagonize him further. She also remembered Ken's words about her learning teamwork, and nodded briskly. "All right. I'll join you there in five minutes."

Sean rose from the chair. "Right."

Lori printed three designs from her disk, and went to his office. He was standing by the drafting board near the window. She spread the small prints over the board. Sean leaned down to look at them. Lori noticed that Sean kept about a foot between them. Well, she had caused this schism. What did she expect?

Sean made a few suggestions to the two designs of the lodge they liked the most and Lori promised to make the changes. He didn't force his ideas on her. He gave her a chance to explain her reasons why she had designed the building the way she had. Then he gave his reasons why the design might not work. He was very much like Ken that way. She understood why Ken had hired him, and thought Sean would probably be a good extension to the firm.

It was mutually decided between Lori, Sean, and Ken that Lori would work on the hotel design and Sean would tackle the separate units. With this decision made, Lori put in long hours for the rest of the week. It was the way she liked her life: busy and occupied. On Saturday she dressed casually in jeans and a blue sweatshirt, and went to the office as usual. Except today Sean would be there.

He was already in, and when Lori went to make some coffee, she discovered he'd made the coffee himself.

"I make it a little weaker than Alan," he said. "I hope that's okay."

She ignored how good he looked in a pair of faded jeans and a black knit sweater. "My insides could do with a rest."

"I know what you mean."

He was looking steadily at her, and Lori became very aware that they were the only two people in the entire building.

"Well," she said, picking up her full mug. "I'll get to work. That's what I'm here for."

"Shall we have pizza delivered for lunch?"

"If you want."

"It means we don't have to stop work for an entire

hour, and anyway it looks as if it's trying to snow again."

Lori peered through the window. The sky was white and a few intermittent flakes were hitting the cold winter ground. "Pizza would be nice. Thank you. I'll give you some money."

"Don't worry. My treat."

"Oh, I. . . ."

"Lori. Why can't you just accept that I want to buy you pizza?" He blew an exasperated puff of air from between his lips.

"Because . . ."

"You think I'm acting like your boss, is that it?"

"Yes. That's it," she said truthfully.

"I thought we were through with all that. I thought we were going to work as a team."

"We are. Aren't we?"

"I'm trying to, Lori, but you are testing my patience." He raked his fingers through his hair. "I don't care that you're a woman. It doesn't make any difference to me when I'm working with you, other than . . ." He placed his hands flat on the counter and drew in a deep breath.

Other than what?

He looked quite haggard as he looked at her. "Okay. When I phone for the pizza, I'll let you know the cost so you can pay me half. That suit you?"

What could she say now, but, "Yes, that suits me."

"Great."

Lori escaped to her office. She was furious with herself. She had messed up again. Or was it all her fault? Maybe he resented having to share his work with *her*. Maybe that's what he was going to say: *Other than I hate working with you.*

Sean called her about an hour later with the amount of money. She took the money from her wallet, walked through to his office, and placed the cash on his desk.

"Thank you," he said, not looking away from his computer screen.

She returned to her own desk and worked through until lunch time. She heard the pizza delivery arrive, and Sean walked by carrying a super huge pizza box. "Shall we eat in the kitchen?"

"All right." She wasn't looking forward to being with him again. There seemed to be a lot of friction between them. Not all of it was work related on her side. She did find him terribly attractive and she was fighting those feelings all the time.

Sean had also ordered a couple of cans of soda pop. They sat down at the kitchen table opposite one another.

He popped the top of his can. "Any problems with George's changes?"

Lori was pleased to talk about work. She had a number of issues she needed to talk to him about, and they came up with some solutions. The napkins were used as sketching paper. As they worked, Lori actually admitted to herself that she valued Sean's opinion and help on the job. Ken wasn't as easy to pin down as Sean was. Sean was much more patient and she actually enjoyed the intellectual interplay. When she was adamant about her design decision he could see her point without having additional explanations. She liked that about him. In fact, she found him quite likeable altogether.

When they finished eating, Sean rose and disposed of the pizza box. "Now the office smells like a restaurant," he said.

"It often does," she told him, rising from her chair, holding her drink. "Thanks for your help."

"I'm learning from you as well, Lori. It's not all one-sided."

She hadn't thought that he might think she knew some things he didn't. "I hope I can be helpful."

"You are helpful." He grinned. "When you're not worrying about your gender. I see you as equal, nothing less."

"Maybe right now, but you're here for a promotion."

"Not for a few years. First of all I have to prove myself."

She hadn't thought about that. "I suppose you do."

"Definitely, I do. And you might not even be here then. So don't cross your bridges before you come to them, as my mother used to tell me when I was over-anxious."

Lori smiled. "My mother said that as well. She still does."

He laughed. "So are we squared?"

She nodded and walked to the door. "Are you coming in to the office tomorrow?"

"No. I'm not. I have something personal lined up tomorrow."

"I do, too," she said, remembering the promised visit to her parents' house.

"Then I'll see you on Monday."

"Yes. Monday."

Back in her office, Lori stared at the screen for a long time without moving. What was really happening between them?

Sean came by when he left to tell her he was leaving.

"Don't work too long," he said. "I've locked up everything. You'll just have to deal with the front door."

"It's fine. I have a key. And I'm finishing up now anyway."

"Good. Have a nice evening."

"And you," she told him, adding a cool smile, wondering what he did on Saturday evenings. Would he go on a date? What was his personal business he had for Sunday?

Lori glanced out of her window and saw Sean walk across the parking lot. It was almost dark. She might as well go home as well. So she packed up and left to go home to a Saturday night alone. Saturday nights alone had never bothered her before she met Sean. Tonight she experienced great pangs of loneliness. She decided to call Susan.

"Do you want to go to a movie?" Lori asked her friend.

"Love to, just to get out of my apartment. How's your man problem?"

"I'll tell you about him."

The movie, the meal afterwards, Susan's company, helped to rid Lori of her loneliness, but because she talked about Sean most of the evening, she couldn't stop herself from thinking about him.

By Sunday, when Lori made the promised visit to her parents, she was getting quite agitated with her inability to push Sean to the back of her mind.

Monday's snowfall had been piled neatly on either side of the wide drive to her parents' house and was as white and pure as the stucco exterior of the home. She always felt as if she were coming home when she visited, but she often wondered if she should have left Ashton Heights when she obtained her degree and gone to live in a larger city where she didn't have to deal with the closeness of a small town.

Slinging with her purse over her shoulder, she walked up the rounded white steps and found the front door open. She pushed on the door, calling for her mother.

Her mother, wearing a blue apron over black slacks

and a pink shirt, bustled from the kitchen. "Hi, Lori. Are you here for lunch?"

Lori took off her black quilted jacket she wore with sweatshirt and jeans. "I guess I am if it's lunchtime. How are you?"

Alice tucked a blonde hair into her upswept style. "Flustered. I have four cats in the garage, where it's too cold to keep them, so your father is trying to funnel heat from the cellar."

"Nothing changes around here."

"I wouldn't want it any other way. Come, follow me to the kitchen. I'm baking muffins."

Lori walked into the warm fragrant kitchen and put her purse down on a kitchen chair. Alice loved baking. There were hot muffins and a pie cooling on racks on the center island.

"Looks wonderful," Lori said.

"Have a muffin, if you want."

Lori put a muffin on a plate. She sat on a chair, broke the muffin apart, and bit a piece off the top. "Chocolate chip. Great."

"I knew you liked those. Here's your Dad."

Jack was well over six foot, broad-shouldered; a comfortable man with gray hair and a small beard. He patted his daughter's shoulder and went to wash his hands at the sink.

"The heat's in the garage," he told his wife. He glanced over his shoulder at Lori. "How's the architectural business?"

"We're busy."

"That's good. Keeps you out of mischief."

"Lori's not the daughter who ever got into mischief," Alice said with a smile. "That one is coming home on Tuesday."

"True." Jack dried his hands. "Lori's our control-freak daughter."

Lori frowned. "I'm not a control-freak."

"You like order, then."

"I might aspire to order, but I don't achieve it. I'm hopelessly out of order. I always seem to be sleeping in and rushing around. My office is a mess. My house is tidy because I have no furniture."

"And you have a new man," her mother said.

Jack reached for a muffin. "Don't these look good. Lori, you try too hard. Just take life as it comes. You've got the degree you wanted. And who is this new man? Don't tell me you have a boyfriend at last?"

Alice jabbed her husband's arm. "I mean the new architect Ken has hired, Jack. Remember?"

"Oh. All that fuss last weekend. I remember. Has he turned out okay, Lori?"

"We're getting used to one another."

"Good. But if you have any problems, I can always talk to Ken."

"Don't you dare. I'll do any necessary talking to Ken. I wish you didn't know everyone in my business."

"I'm *in* your business."

"Which is where you got the building bug from," Alice inserted. "Why didn't you become a vet? I could have done with a vet in the family."

Lori laughed. "You should have had a third daughter for that."

"Two is plenty." Alice put out some sandwiches on a plate. "Now eat up."

As her mother spoke, a meow made Lori look down at the gray cat, Parker, who was hovering around her feet. "He doesn't like muffins, does he?"

Alice chuckled. "He likes everything. Give him a crumb."

Lori fed a crumb of muffin to the cat at her feet, who promptly sat down underneath her chair. Three more cats strolled in. Only Parker, and a female calico named Polly were the actual family cats. The rest were transitory. They changed from week to week, month to month, year to year. Rarely were only Parker and Polly resident.

After they finished sandwiches, muffins and coffee, Lori went with her father to inspect his plans for the bedrooms he was enlarging. He was adding adjoining bathrooms to both.

"Looks good," Lori said as she read his crude plans. "But it means Julie has to stay with me."

"You can keep an eye on her."

"She's almost thirty, Dad."

"I know. Old enough to be married and settled down with some kids."

"Julie's never been that type."

"Neither have you," her father said. "Oh, well."

But Lori knew there was sadness in that "oh, well." Her parents would like grandchildren. Kids would add to the chaos they seemed to love and feed off of in their life.

As she drove home she wished she had a sister who had complied with these desires, so she would be left free of guilt. But it wasn't her fault her parents had produced two independent women, who hadn't yet found the loves of their lives.

And probably never would, she decided, as she sat at her computer later in the afternoon working on the Hinton design in her nice quiet space upstairs. She felt at her most comfortable working. She certainly hadn't felt comfortable this week. And she blamed the uneasiness on Sean. She hoped next week she would see Sean in a different light; a neutral light.

Chapter Four

By Monday morning, Lori had designed the ski resort hotel in every possible way. She went to work,
looking forward to showing Sean her designs. When
she discovered he wasn't there, she felt cheated. She
was sure he had told her he would see her on Monday.
Eventually she saw Ken in the kitchen and asked
where Sean was.

Ken poured himself some coffee. "Oh, he had to go
back to arrange the move of his belongings to Ashton
Heights. He was in a rented house and thought he had
it for longer, but the landlord managed to rent it again
early. So, Sean has to get out. He'll be back tomorrow." Ken gave her a crooked grin. "Why?"

"Oh. He . . . er, told me he was going to be here

today, and I had something to discuss with him. It can wait." She smiled and picked up her coffee mug.

But back in her office she stormed around. All Sunday afternoon and evening she had slaved on designs to show George at the Tuesday meeting. Without Sean around to discuss them, she might not have them ready for the meeting after all. She hated going to meetings unprepared, especially meetings with George.

She knew she was upset because she had worked so hard and she wanted Sean's approval. *You're being childish, Lori! This is work. This is business. It's not play. You know you are a good architect. You know what works in design. You don't need his approval. Take charge, woman.*

So she took charge, finished the designs and put a set of prints in Sean's office with a note.

She went home right at five o'clock, so that she could prepare the house for Julie's arrival tomorrow. Once home, Lori changed into jeans and a denim shirt, ate a quick microwaved dinner, and dragged the vacuum cleaner upstairs to the bedroom Julie would be staying in. As she pushed the vacuum cleaner backwards and forwards on the pale blue rug, she realized that work hadn't been the same without Sean today. She had missed the man and that wasn't what she wanted.

When she had finished cleaning the room, Julie phoned.

"I'm flying home tomorrow, kid. Dad's going to pick me up in Buffalo. I'll go home first to dump some belongings, and then he'll bring me to your place. Okay?"

Lori tucked a hunk of hair back behind her ear. "How many belongings do you have?"

"I'm coming back East for good. So everything I took with me and more is coming with me."

"But you're going to New York?"

"Oh, yes."

"That's fine then, Julie."

"You don't sound as if these arrangements are cool with you, Lori."

"It's cool with me. I'm just busy at work, that's all."

"I won't get in your way. Promise."

Lori suddenly wondered if she had hurt her sister. "I want you to stay, Julie. Really."

"Good, because I want to stay with you. We haven't been alone together for years."

"That's true."

"I'll see you tomorrow, then," Julie said.

Lori found she woke up the next morning feeling excited because she was seeing Julie. At least Julie's arrival overshadowed some of her feelings for Sean, she decided on the way to work.

She was just taking off her coat in her office when Sean came in.

"Hi, Lori. Sorry I wasn't here yesterday. An emergency cropped up."

She hung her coat over the hanger. "Yes, I heard. Ken explained."

"Did you get anything ready to show George at the meeting?"

"Definitely. I've left some copies of my drawings on your board, so you can have a peek before we leave. How was your trip downstate to upstate?"

He laughed. "It was fine. Ken probably told you, the room at my hotel runs out soon. I had to get the movers to come yesterday and pick up my stuff. It's going into storage until I find a new place."

"Are you going to rent again?"

He pushed his hands into the pockets of his black slacks. "No. I think I'll buy something. It's about time I settled down."

"You're not the settling down type?"

"I've always been a bit of a wanderlust. I spent some of my study time over in Europe. I took a year off as well and went to Asia."

"And you end up in Ashton Heights."

"Nothing wrong with it here, Lori. Don't you like it?"

"Yes. I like it very much. Otherwise I wouldn't be here."

"Believe me the air is sweeter here." He smiled. "I'll go look at those designs before the meeting. I've got some errands to run after the meeting, so if you don't mind meeting me there, it would help."

Lori hadn't realized how much she had been looking forward to driving to the ski resort with Sean. Suddenly her day had lost its glitter. Outside, she noticed snowflakes hurling down from the sky. "Fine," she said quickly with a bright smile. She didn't want every move Sean made to affect her moods.

As soon as Sean was gone, Lori hoped Sean's decision to take separate transportation hadn't been influenced by her behavior last week. She made up her mind, once again, to be only businesslike with him. She needed to reverse any negative opinions he might have of her.

Lori met Sean outside George's office. They had a brief meeting and left the designs with George who was going to look carefully at each one and show them to his wife when she came home this week. Lori went back to the office, while Sean went to see a company about his storage facilities.

Because Julie was expected, Lori had to leave the office right at five. Her father's red truck was already outside her house. As soon as Lori drove into her driveway, Julie alighted, wearing a silver leather jacket and jeans. Her golden hair had been cut short.

Lori realized she hadn't seen Julie since before she had moved into this house and she felt tears fill her eyes. They ran to one another and hugged.

"It's good to see you, Lori," Julie said. "I've missed you."

"I've missed you as well," Lori admitted. "Your hair looks really cute."

Julie touched her head. "It feels very short. Yours is still long?"

"Yes. I can't seem to part with it." Lori laughed.

Lori unlocked the front door. Her father and Julie hauled in three suitcases and a guitar case from the back of the truck.

"I'll be off," her father said. "I have a meeting in ten minutes with Ken."

Lori wanted to ask her father what his meeting with Ken was about but he was already out the door and on his way to the truck.

Lori closed the door and looked at Julie. "So you're here."

Julie grinned. "Yes. I'm here."

Lori picked up one of the suitcases. "I've put you in the back bedroom at the top. It's the only room. I use the second bedroom as an office."

Julie followed her upstairs with more luggage. "This is a great place. I've never been in one of these town-houses, but I've always admired them."

Lori began to climb the second flight of stairs to the third floor.

"Another flight of stairs. Wow. I bet the view is good."

"It is." Lori pushed on the door to Julie's room. "How's this?"

Julie tossed her bag on the floor. "A bed. Great."

"Sorry, there's not much furniture. I haven't been able to afford much."

"I can understand that. Do you have any drawers?"

Lori flung open the closet door. The closet was like a room. There were shelves and drawer space built in. "How's that?"

"Hey, great. Would you mind if I brought over an armchair and my desk from home?"

"If you can get Dad to bring them over. But it's only for a couple of weeks, isn't it? So why bother?"

"Because I'll need a chair and desk even for only a few weeks."

The time had been extended to a *few* weeks now, Lori thought.

Julie peered from the window. "Ah, the ski slopes. I think I'll ski while I'm home."

"Julie, Mom and Dad hate you skiing."

Julie turned around and made a face. "I know. My leg still feels stiff at times from breaking it in high school."

"Then don't do it. I've never skied."

"Because you aren't adventurous, Lori. Don't you even have a boyfriend?"

"No, but neither do you."

Julie sat down on the bed and dangled her long fingers between her knees. Her fingernails were painted purple. "Half the reason I came back is that my romance ended."

Lori looked at her sister's forlorn features. "Were you in love with him?"

"I thought so. His name is Carson Taylor. He's a music exec. Bad choice for a struggling no-name wannabe, I know, but that's the way things went."

"Why did you break up?"

"It just didn't work out."

"That's not a very good answer."

"Well, it's the only one I know." Julie smiled at her sister. "But I'm okay about it. Part of the reason we broke up is because I wasn't ready for the huge commitment of marriage."

"That's a good reason."

"It is." Julie stood up. "Do you want to go out for dinner? My treat."

Lori supposed they could. She didn't have much in her refrigerator.

"What about Mom and Dad?" she asked.

"We're going there tomorrow evening. Mother's busy with a meeting tonight."

It seemed Lori's life was being planned for her. Still, she could survive a couple of weeks or so. "All right. Let's go out to eat."

Lori changed into jeans. Then she drove to The Heights, Julie's choice of restaurant.

"Ooh a new fireplace," Julie said as they walked into the low-lit interior.

"It's *apres-ski* everything now," Lori told her. "As if nothing else happens here."

"Some people would believe nothing else does happen here," Julie commented, glancing around at the patrons. "I don't think I know anyone in this town anymore."

"All those new houses on the outskirts have attracted new residents," Lori said. "But it's still a very small place."

"Small-minded still?"

Lori smiled. "That, too."

"Oh, well, I'm off to New York City soon. This is just a stopover. You should come with me."

Maybe when Julie was settled, she might go and look for a job in New York. It was a possibility, an idea to be explored. Certainly her current job wasn't in the same comfort zone since Sean's arrival.

A hostess showed them to a window booth. Lori looked at the menu, remembering the last time she had been here with Sean. She wished his name didn't keep sliding into her consciousness.

Lori chose grilled fish, a baked potato, and a salad to eat. When she put down her menu, she noticed that Julie hadn't even opened hers yet. She was staring across the restaurant to another booth.

Julie leaned over the table and said softly, "I know that guy."

Lori turned around and saw Sean sitting in a booth alone. Her heart began to pound, but she didn't think Julie meant Sean. She couldn't possibly know him. There were a number of other men: two muscular men with short hair, in jeans and check shirts, who looked like football players; and a tall thin man in a suit with two women who looked like real estate agents. "Which guy?"

"The one alone in the booth. He lived in Ellis Corners when I was in high school."

Lori couldn't believe Julie had pinpointed Sean. "I don't think you do know him, Julie."

"Yes, I do. His name is Sean Matheson."

"He's an architect," Lori said. "He's from New York City."

"You know him?"

"He just came to work for Ken. But he's never mentioned he's from around here."

"He definitely is. He played football for Ellis High."

"So that's how you know him. You were a cheerleader for Ashton High, weren't you?"

"Yes. A bunch of us used to get together after the games and Sean was one of them."

"Great," Lori said. "Here's me thinking he's "big city" and he's from only twenty miles down the highway."

"What difference does it make?"

"It makes a lot of difference." Lori thought about her comments on his shoes. *Argh.*

"Can I call him over then?" Julie asked.

"Oh, Julie."

"The reason I've stopped off here for a while is to see old friends."

Julie began to try to catch Sean's attention. Eventually she did. Surreptitiously, Lori glanced over her shoulder and saw Sean smile with recognition. So he did know Julie. She saw him leave a tip and pick up his check, but instead of going to the cash register, he walked their way. Under his leather jacket he was wearing a gray T-shirt and the snug faded jeans he'd worn to work last Saturday. Lori had never seen him look so attractive. There was a prowl to his walk and a greater width to his chest and shoulders than she'd noticed at the office. She tried to imagine him in the Ellis High yellow and purple football colors and it really wasn't difficult.

"Hey, Julie," he said, shaking Julie's hand. "I haven't seen you for years, and I . . ." He glanced down at Lori. ". . . I never connected the Fenton name with Lori."

"She's my little sister," Julie said. "Join us?"

Lori grimaced at Julie calling her "little." She hoped Sean would decline the invitation.

It sounded as if he might, as he said, "It's okay. I've already eaten. In fact, I've eaten here every night since Lori introduced me to the place on my first day." He smiled at Lori.

Lori forced a smile. "I'm pleased I could be of help."

Julie tugged on his jacket by the zipper. "Have another coffee. I'm only in town for a few weeks. Maybe we can arrange something with the old gang."

Lori didn't enjoy seeing Julie's fingers pulling at Sean's jacket. Jealousy surged through her. She clenched her hands beneath the table and her nails scraped her palm. She *wasn't* falling in love with Sean. She wasn't.

"Where have you been living?" Sean asked Julie.

Lori could see by his expression that he thought Julie was very attractive.

Julie was looking up at Sean. "L.A. But I'm moving to New York. I'm visiting family on the way. In fact, I'm staying with Lori."

"That's great." Sean glanced over at Lori again. "Okay. I'll have another cup of coffee and maybe some of that pecan pie I told myself I couldn't get down five minutes ago."

Sean tucked himself into the booth beside Julie, so he was right opposite Lori, and much too close to her sister for her peace of mind. She felt like taking her big leather purse and putting it between them on the seat to keep them apart.

Julie ordered the same meal as Lori. Sean ordered another coffee with his pie, and asked the waitress to add everything to his current check.

Lori gazed at him as he spoke to the waitress. His hair was tousled this evening and his jaw was a little bristly. He looked casual and completely at ease.

"It's okay if I pay, Lori?" Sean asked. "I'm not trying to be the boss or anything. We're outside of work."

Lori wished he hadn't referred to the pizza incident. Julie was looking at them with intense interest.

"It's fine," she said abruptly, feeling her cheeks flush.

Julie laughed. "What's all this about?"

"It's just a joke," Sean said. "Something at work between Lori and me."

"You have time for jokes at work? I thought Lori was particularly serious about her career."

Sean kept one eye on Lori as he spoke. "She is. Extremely serious."

Lori's agitation rose, but she kept a calm façade. "This has nothing to do with the question at hand." She smiled at Sean. "I'll accept your offer of dinner. Thank you."

"You're welcome." He winked at her to ease her tension.

Lori sat back against her seat and breathed out.

Julie adjusted her back to the wall, so she was facing Sean. Sean turned around on the bench seat, his arm along the top, his hand almost touching Julie's shoulder.

What if Sean and Julie began to date?

"So what brings you back to the area?" Julie asked Sean.

Lori listened attentively as he told Julie he had grown weary of city living. Besides, there had been no chance for advancement at his previous firm. Here, there was the chance of a partnership, either before or after Ken retired. Also, Sean's father had recently died and he wanted to be closer to his mother in Ellis Corners. There were no architectural firms in Ellis Corners so Ken's advertisement in an industry magazine seemed like the perfect opportunity.

"It's great," Julie told him. "Lori loves working for Ken, don't you?"

"I've enjoyed it, yes," she said carefully.

Sean glanced at her. "Lori's a good architect. She just whipped up some great designs for the new ski lodge."

Her skin warmed up with Sean's unexpected praise. "Oh, yes. I just whipped them up."

"You know what I mean," Sean said.

He was now facing Lori again. His nice hands with long lean fingers and blunt fingernails were resting on the table.

Lori could barely eat anything. She picked at the dinner and nibbled on a roll. She let Julie and Sean do most of the talking. They chatted about old times— football, mostly.

When they finished and were ready to go, Sean walked with them to Lori's car. Julie thanked him profusely for paying for their dinner. Lori wished he hadn't, but she wasn't going to make a fuss.

"It was my pleasure, Julie," he said. "I hope to see you again?"

"Yes. We'll get together." Julie touched his jacket.

Sean seemed to lean a little closer to her sister. Lori rattled her car keys. "Shall we get going? It's cold. It's late. And I have to work tomorrow."

"It is cold," Sean said. "Real great seeing you again, Julie. Lori, see you tomorrow."

Sean kissed Julie's cheek. Lori turned away and opened the car door. When she looked up again, Sean was striding over the parking lot and Julie was waiting for the passenger door to be unlocked.

"You have quite a relationship with Sean," Julie said as Lori drove home.

"I don't know what you mean."

"I mean that you're tense with him."

Lori tried to think of an excuse. It was a legitimate one. "He never told me he was from Ellis Corners. I presumed he was New York City, born and bred, and I made some gaffes."

"What kind of gaffes?"

Lori explained the shoe incident.

Julie chuckled. "So you've got off on the wrong foot with Sean?"

"You could say that," Lori admitted. "But we're fine when it comes to working together."

Julie twisted in the seat. "Then what's the problem? Knowing Sean, I would think the shoe episode would only be a giggle."

Lori couldn't imagine Sean giggling but she had to admit that now she knew he was from a nearby town, he probably *had* shrugged off the episode. He wasn't a big city guy; He was a local guy. He had no reason to feel put down. "I suppose there really isn't any problem."

"Are you sure? I know I had a crush on him the first time I met him."

That was information Lori didn't want to know. She clutched the steering wheel. The snow during the day had stopped and melted on the roads. Neon lights flashed colored streaks on the pavement before her eyes.

"Do *you* have a crush on him?" Julie asked.

"Oh, no." Lori opted for another excuse. "I'm just aggravated over that chance for advancement he mentioned."

"Well, the guy has to have a future."

"I realize that. And Ken's not retiring right away either, but still he's come in and taken over in some respects."

"Has Ken demoted you?"

"Not officially."

"But you feel demoted?"

"Yes."

Julie sighed. "Why don't you speak to Ken about it?"

"I have in some respects. Ken thinks I should learn teamwork."

"Well, maybe you need to. Lori, even though you're my younger sister, you've always been more dominant. Maybe you need to back off. Ken hasn't retired yet, so don't make life hard for yourself just because of something that might or might not happen. Sean's a nice guy and I'm sure you'll be fine working with him once you get used to it."

"I'm not disputing that he's a nice guy, Julie. And I'm fine working with him."

Julie let out an exasperated sigh. "Then what are you disputing? I'm getting the impression we're talking in circles."

Lori drove into her driveway and picked up the remote to open the garage door.

"You *do* have a crush on him."

Lori was glad it was dark in the garage, but the light remained on inside the car for a moment and Julie was staring at her.

"You do, don't you?"

Lori brushed back her hair from her face. "I don't know."

"I can fully understand if you do; he's a cutie. But not my type, I'll add, so don't go getting jealous or anything. He's just a friend in my camp."

Lori shrugged. "It doesn't really matter."

"Oh, yes it does. I don't want you thinking I'm out to grab Sean from you. I'm not. And I won't."

"But you had a crush on him once."

"Nothing serious, believe me."

"What put you off him?" Lori hoped he had a bad habit that would turn her off him as well.

"Another boyfriend, who I fell madly in love with. Sean was just a brief crush. He didn't even know."

"That's how it will probably be for me," Lori said.

"Maybe. Maybe not. He seemed to like you. He looked at you a lot."

Lori removed her keys from the ignition. "I don't know about that. Anyway, I don't want to fall in love. I want to set up my own business first. I don't want to be married and raising children at the same time. I certainly don't want to get attached to Sean in the office. I want everything to be peaceful."

"Life isn't fun if it's peaceful," Julie said.

"She proclaims in all her infinite wisdom."

"Well, I am older than you. And I have been in love more."

Lori bowed her head. "I suppose."

"If you want what you say you want, then you have to give up love for a while," Julie said.

Lori glanced at her. "Is that what you've done with Carson?"

Julie nodded. "I have too many things to do right now."

"That's exactly how I feel, Julie. I didn't think we were alike."

"Well, we are, somewhat." Julie opened her door and climbed out of the car.

Lori was relieved when Julie said she felt tired and went to her room. Lori took a shower and put on black leggings and an oversize white fleecy sweatshirt. She walked into her office and sat down at her computer, but didn't turn the machine on. She could barely think straight, so how could she work? She might as well set up the kitchen for tomorrow morning's breakfast and then go to bed herself.

Except she didn't fall asleep. She kept seeing Sean; the first day in his black suit and tonight in his black leather jacket and snug jeans, his hair a little tousled, his jaw a little unshaven. . . . She buried her face in the pillow. *Oh, no, oh, no, oh, no.*

Chapter Five

Lori barely slept. She missed her alarm and was ten minutes late to work. She crept past Mary talking on the phone. Luckily Bob and Alan weren't at their computers to remark upon her lateness, so she was able to scurry through their office. She quickly shed her coat and turned on her computer.

"Good morning, Lori." Sean rested one hand against the edge of her partition. In the other, he was carrying an empty black mug.

Sean was the last person she needed to see this morning. She was still shaken from seeing him last night. It also didn't help that he looked so good either: clean-shaven, wearing black pants, black shirt, and silver tie. However, his hair still looked tousled like last night, as if he had raked his fingers through it a few times. She also thought his eyes looked tired.

She straightened her shoulders. "Hi. I see you're getting used to the office coffee."

He lifted his mug. "I made a deal with Alan that he would make it a little weaker."

Lori wondered how Alan had taken that instruction. It helped her to keep thinking of Sean as the interloper.

Sean walked into her office and came closer to the desk. "Did you know I was once a friend of Julie's; I mean, before last night?"

She shook her head. "No, I had no idea. I didn't know you were from around here. I don't know why you didn't tell me."

He let out a breath. "I didn't think it was necessary. But obviously it is. And now you know I am, things can settle down, can't they?"

"You mean my comments about your shoes and your vehicle?"

"Among other things. I've come home, and as this is the only architectural firm within a radius of fifty miles, I've come to work here. And I don't have to apologize for any of that."

"I don't expect you to apologize for it, Sean. But you let me think you were from the city."

"I suppose I did."

"You wanted me to think that, didn't you?"

"If you had known I was from the Corners you would have dismissed me."

"What do you mean?"

He grinned. "I'm more formidable if I'm from the city."

Lori laughed. "You wanted me to think you were formidable?"

"Not really formidable, but I wanted to make an impression. You must have wanted to make an impression on me."

"I did, didn't I? A negative one."

"I don't think it was negative. You acted in perfect accordance with the situation."

"Predictable?"

"You could say that."

"And you could have eased things by telling me the truth."

"I suppose. Anyway," he stepped even closer to her. "Shall we call a truce?"

"I didn't think we were at war."

"Not exactly at war, but we haven't been in harmony."

"I didn't mean it to be that way."

"I know, and I understand, really, I do. I would feel the same way if I was here first."

"I don't know if you would."

"I would. I know I would. I'm soft inside."

He had made himself vulnerable to her. Whether or not all this was blatant manipulation or the truth, Lori knew she had to grab her chance to start afresh. She pushed back her chair and stood up. She offered her hand to him. "Okay. Truce."

He shook her hand, his fingers firm, warm, and compelling. She didn't want to let go. She wanted him to hold on and draw her closer to him.

Still holding hands, they locked gazes. The green of Sean's eyes reminded Lori of fresh spring mornings. She felt Sean's grip tighten slightly. She swallowed hard. The room seemed to be spinning. Then Sean let her fingers slide very slowly from his. When they lost contact, they were still looking at one another.

Lori turned away and began to fiddle with some papers on her desk. "I had better get to work." She needed to clear her head, so she tossed her hair over her shoulders.

Sean moved away from her. "I also need to fill this coffee mug before the coffee gets stale." He let out a short breath. "See you later, Lori."

When he was gone, Lori closed her eyes for a second. Then she sat down on her chair with a crash. She remembered the jealousy she experienced last night with Julie and Sean across from her in the restaurant booth. She remembered lying in bed last night with her face buried in the pillow, wondering what was happening to her. She wasn't falling in love with him. She couldn't be. Whatever it was that was making her feel this way, she would get over it. She would.

Lori opened her front door, stepped over a box and

banged her shin against a TV set. She heard Julie's feet scampering down her stairs. Dressed in slim jeans and a T-shirt, her sister held something in her arms.

"What is that?" Lori asked, not bothering to take off her coat as she vaulted across more clutter.

Julie held up a black-and-white year-old feline. "A cat named Fran. It fights with the other cats, so mother suggested I look after it for the few weeks I'm here. By the time I leave, she should have a home for it."

Lori glanced around. She really was at the end of her tether. "Julie. You're overstepping the mark here. Look at all this."

"Don't have a tantrum, Lori. I need a TV in my room. Dad let me have an old color portable from their bedroom. And the boxes hold my songwriting stuff. Dad put the desk and armchair upstairs today."

"This is *my* house, Julie."

"I know, and it's kind of you to let me stay, but it's only for a few weeks."

"I thought it was two."

"Three at the most, Lori."

"Well, as long as it's only three." Lori sighed. "I work at home. I need peace and quiet. That's why I moved away from mom and dad."

"I know. I'll be really quiet. I'm getting in touch with a lot of friends, so I'll be going out a lot. For instance, I'll be away this weekend."

Lori remembered Ken's party this weekend. She was pleased Julie would be away. Julie would make a thing of her going to a party that was to be attended by Sean.

Fran meowed. "And I hope you'll look after the cat? I'm not here all day."

Julie nodded. "Will do." She let Fran down. Fran ran into the kitchen. "I put her food in the kitchen and her litter box down in the basement. All right?"

Instead of letting the rising scream escape, Lori nodded. She side stepped the clutter and took off her coat and hung it up. "I'll help you get this stuff upstairs. Is there a spot for the TV in your room?"

"Yep. Dad fixed it. We just have to plug it in. He had to leave for a meeting, otherwise he would have finished carrying this stuff up." Julie moved forward. "Lori, I understand why you feel you can't have any noise, I really do, but . . . I think I'm more like Mom. I thrive on chaos. It causes tension and I write better."

"Not me. I'm like Grandad. He likes quiet."

"Which is why Gramma is out volunteering all the time. She likes uproar."

"Because Gramma is like her daughter, our mother."

Julie chuckled. "I don't know why you want to separate yourself from your family, Lori. We're all you have."

"I know. And I love you all dearly. I'm not separating myself. I just have a career to get started and I can't do that with continual hassles and interruptions. That's all."

"But you still can't get up in the mornings. I heard you rushing about this morning."

Lori dragged her fingers through her hair. "I suppose you're still an early riser?"

"Absolutely. I stayed out of your way this morning, but I'll make sure you're up from now on. I'll earn my keep."

Lori picked up a box and began to walk up the stairs with it. "I'll remember you said that."

Julie followed with the TV set. This evening they had to go to Mom and Dad's for dinner. Lori was beginning to wonder if Hinton's Ski Lodge would ever get out of the design stage, let alone be built.

Julie banged on her door the next morning before the alarm. Lori muttered under her breath but then smelled the lovely aroma of coffee floating up the stairs. She slid out of bed and wrapped herself in a warm robe. Fran came up the stairs to greet her so Lori scooped up the little cat and walked down to the kitchen.

Julie was dressed in yellow leggings and a green sweatshirt.

"Wow. You're bright in the morning." Lori shielded her eyes as she let Fran go to her food dish. "You look like a football team."

"These were my cheerleading colors. What do you want for breakfast?"

Lori picked up a glass of orange juice that had been set in her place. "I don't eat breakfast."

"You have to eat breakfast in cold weather. Have some cereal. You've got plenty of time."

Lori glanced at the microwave clock and saw that it was only six o'clock. "It's so early."

"Which means you have plenty of time for breakfast. I'll slice you up some fruit to go with your cereal."

Lori sat in her chair. "Since when did you get so domesticated?"

"Since always. I'm like Mom. Remember?"

"I suppose I do." Lori felt as if she had been distancing herself from her family for a long time. Architectural study had been absorbing, including a six-month term in Italy. Her job was usually absorbing as well. Except right now she was distracted by Sean.

Sean wasn't in the office when Lori got there and Lori was pleased. She had to work. And work she did. She managed to stay at the computer all morning, with only one break for coffee. For lunch she heated a frozen lasagna Julie had made her take with her. She ate it while working at her desk. By the end of the day she felt as if she had finally accomplished something.

The only sour note of her day was that she hadn't seen Sean. As she left with Mary and they walked across the parking lot to their cars, Mary told her that Sean had called to say he was away on business for the day.

"What business?"

"I don't know. He just said business."

"And you didn't ask where he could be reached?"

"Of course I did. I'm efficient. He said he would call in on his cell phone and I could give that number to anyone in an emergency. But he hasn't been with us long enough to have emergencies. You can handle George Hinton's calls."

Of course. Sean had Lori back at the office slaving away on the job he would probably end up getting the credit for.

Lori drove home feeling sorry for herself. Or was she feeling sorry because she hadn't seen Sean all day? She really didn't know, and didn't want to analyze her feelings too closely.

Julie had dinner ready and they ate it together in the kitchen. Having Julie around was rather like having her mom around again, Lori decided. She had always thought of her sister as a rather self-interested type of woman who relied on others for her comforts, but Julie was showing a new side of herself.

When Lori left for work in the morning, Julie was vacuuming.

"Are you just doing this to earn your keep or are you really like this now?" she asked as she put on her coat.

Julie turned off the switch. "I'm like this. But I also want to earn my keep. As soon as you're gone I'm going to start some songwriting."

"Have a good day, then," Lori told her.

The party was the talk of the office; everyone was

bringing a food dish to add to the buffet the following evening. Mary and her husband, Paul, would be there; so would Jennifer and her boyfriend; Bob and Louise; and Alan and his girlfriend, Mara. Peter and Lynn Rhodes would probably be there as well. And if Sean brought someone with him—just because he wasn't married, didn't mean he couldn't bring a date—then she would be the odd one out. She hadn't thought of that possibility, and wondered about calling John Styles, an engineer she had dated about a year ago. Then she decided that was silly. She hadn't liked him enough to keep the relationship going before, so why now? Her ambivalence about him was the reason they weren't dating anymore.

She saw Sean around the office a couple of times, but they were both extremely busy, and there just wasn't the opportunity to discuss the party. She figured he probably would bring a date.

On Saturday evening, Lori chose to be optimistic about the staff party, telling herself the event was for her career, not her personal life. She dressed in black silk flowing pants, and a silver halter top with a sheer black blouse overtop. She coiled her hair upon her head, added silver earrings and slipped her feet into a pair of black patent leather shoes. Finally she put on her black coat, picked up the salad she was bringing, and went out to her car to drive to Ken's home.

The Randall's house was built on about four acres.

Ken had designed the home himself after he became married with two small children. It was an interesting home on a number of floor levels with pale wood of all angles and peaks. The front door was placed down a few steps.

Caroline, wearing dark green pants and top, was a plump, dark-haired easygoing woman. Once a school-teacher, she spent most of her time now either helping Ken at the office, or looking after her grandchildren while her two daughters worked. Her teenage son was still in high school and was the one who came into the office to work.

"How are you, Lori?" Caroline asked as she took her coat from her.

"I'm fine, Caroline. How are you?"

"Couldn't be better. I understand we're going to meet the new man tonight."

"He's not here yet?"

"No. Ken said he might be delayed as he was fixing a deal to buy a house. One of yours."

Lori felt her throat dry up as she followed Caroline to the kitchen to put her salad in the refrigerator. "Do you mean he's moving into one of the townhouses I live in?"

Caroline made room on a fridge shelf. "Yes. A couple of your townhouses were up for sale, so Sean grabbed one."

Sean was going to live in her condominium development. She was never going to have any distance from him. She couldn't believe it. But then why shouldn't she believe it? Ashton Heights wasn't booming with townhouses. Ken's had been the first development. There had been only one other development since, and it had been built by a contractor as a model design. They were cheaper, without individual designs. Naturally, Sean would want to live in an architecturally-interesting home—especially if the architect he worked for had designed the house. Hadn't she thought the same thing when she had bought her house?

"That will be nice for him," Lori said.

"You don't sound thrilled. Don't you like him?"

Lori knew Caroline would probably tell Ken anything she said, so she smiled brightly. "Oh, yes. I like him."

Caroline laughed. "He's obviously livened up Ken's office. Come on, let's make it known you're here."

Lori followed Caroline up more steps into a large living room, where some of the staff were already gathered.

Lori sat down near Bob and Louise. Louise, a very tall, statuesque woman with long black hair, was pregnant so they talked about babies. But all the while Lori waited for the doorbell to ring. When it did, all her stomach muscles tensed. She knew that she was more in tune with Sean than she ever wanted to be. *And it's only been a couple of weeks. How am I going to feel after a month?*

Mary and Paul came into the living room and Lori swallowed her disappointment. She really was in a bad way.

Paul, a lawyer, was a slightly balding man in a gray suit. Lori had met him a couple of times and knew that he had a keen sense of humor.

"Sean not here yet?" Mary asked Lori, sitting down beside her, while Paul chatted to Ken.

Lori shook her head. "Doesn't seem like it. Apparently, he bought a house today."

"One of yours?"

"You knew he was looking at them?"

"I suggested them when he asked. Ken said there were some for sale."

"Well, it seems that way." Lori sighed.

Mary grinned. "Oh, dear, he's got to you."

"No. No." Lori denied her attraction. "It's just that he's enough at work."

"Are you that friendly with your neighbors?"

"Not really," Lori admitted. On the right, she had a career couple who were never there, and on the left, was a single woman who she saw once in a while for a brief chat. Rarely did she see anyone else in the winter.

"Don't worry about it then." Mary patted her knee.

Peter and Lynn arrived. Lynn was a friend of Caroline's; the two women immediately began chatting about the dish of food Lynn had brought while walking to the kitchen together. After bidding everyone good evening, Peter gravitated with a drink in his hand and to his partner, Ken.

Sean didn't get there until they were setting up the food on the table. Lori hadn't expected him to bring a dish, but he had with him a Black Forest cake from a local bakery. Lori helped him open the package and put the cake on to a plate.

"It looks great," she told him, very aware of him in his black slacks and white sweater.

"What did you bring?"

"I made a salad." She pointed to it. "I won't win Cook of the Year with it, but it's edible."

"It looks good. This hotel thing is all right, but I'm looking forward to getting into my own place with my own kitchen."

Lori adjusted some plastic wrap covering a dish. "Yes, I heard you bought a house today."

"Word sure gets around fast in this town. Yes, I did."

Ken came over to see Sean. Sean shook his boss's hand and told him about the house.

"What number are you, Lori?" Ken asked.

"Forty-eight. What number did you buy, Sean?"

"Forty-five."

"Oh." Sean would only be two doors down from her.

Sean rested his gaze on her. "That's an interesting reaction."

Sean's gaze was warm and mesmerizing. Lori's

heart began to pound of its own accord. "It's one of the corner units," she said. "Larger than mine with a great view."

"The view is what sold me."

"That was my intention," Ken said. "Build them tall and lean." He smiled at them both. "Now I'll go circulate. You two have fun."

Peter Rhodes came over next to see Sean. He had a habit of smoothing his thinning blonde hair as he spoke, and he didn't really say much except for a few comments about the weather.

After Peter drifted away, she turned to Sean. "Well, so much for Peter."

"He bothers you?"

"I barely see him. Did he hire you?"

"No. It was all Ken."

Lori felt she was standing much too close to Sean, but she couldn't help herself. She wanted to be close to him. "Did you have parties in your other firm?"

Sean seemed to move closer to her as well. "Maybe drinks on Friday evening at a pub, but nothing like this. This is downright homey. Potluck supper and everything."

"That's the way it is in this town. Downright homey."

"I know I'm going to enjoy it," he said very softly.

They were very close together now. If Lori moved an inch her arm would touch his. She moved that inch because she couldn't help herself. And she felt the pressure of Sean's arm against hers. She looked at him and his eyes were very dark, like moss. Her mouth trembled.

If Caroline hadn't called out, "Food is served," at that moment Lori wasn't sure what might have happened. She thought he might have kissed her. Although, she knew in reality he wouldn't kiss her in front of everyone. And why should he kiss her? It was she who was infatuated with him, not the other way around.

They both walked over to the table and picked up plates.

There were all sorts of delicacies: shrimp rings, chicken, sausage rolls, miniature quiches, salads, vegetables, casseroles, pasta. Lori chose some of each. So did Sean. While everyone else served themselves as well, Lori and Sean sat down beside one another on a sofa. Lori felt as if she were with him. She wanted to be with him.

"This looks good," Sean said as they dug into the food. "So how is it living in those condos?"

"Great."

"You live alone?"

She nodded. "Yes."

"I wasn't sure. I thought maybe. . . ." He shrugged his shoulders.

Lori got his meaning. He believed she might have a boyfriend. She had never given a moment's thought to him thinking she wasn't single. And yet she had wondered at first if he might be married. Why shouldn't he wonder the same thing about her? "I bought the house about a year ago," she said. "I came back from college and lived with my parents until I found their lifestyle entirely too chaotic."

He smiled. "What do you mean?"

"My father's in construction and he's forever building extensions onto the house. My mother fosters cats until homes are found for them. And you know Julie. She's a musician."

"And you like peace and quiet; is that it?"

"Very much."

"Well, I'm pleased it's a nice quiet development. I'm looking forward to moving in."

"When are you moving?"

"The unit is empty now. Two weeks. At the end of this month."

Lori wasn't sure how she was going to feel when Sean was a couple of houses away from her. She wasn't ever going to get away from him. Her throat felt tight and she almost choked on her food.

Sean handed her a glass. "Drink some of this." He touched her back gently and applied a slight pressure as she drank the soft drink and felt the food dislodge.

"All right now?"

"Thank you. Yes." She placed the glass back on the table. "Something went down the wrong way."

"Poor you." He let his hand drop down her back in a caress.

Lori stiffened under his touch. His fingers felt as if they were scalding her back before he withdrew his hand.

"How are we doing?" Caroline sat down beside Sean on the other side.

They began a conversation about Manhattan and Lori managed to sneak away and put her empty plate in the kitchen. She poured herself some coffee from the coffeemaker. She was sipping from the cup when Bob came in.

"I saw you snuggled up on the couch with Sean," he said, pouring himself some coffee.

"I wasn't *snuggled.*"

"No. But you seem to have smoothed out your differences."

"I apologized," Lori admitted. "And he's not holding a grudge against me."

"I guess not. He's from Ellis Corners, originally. Did you know that?"

"I do now," she said a little sheepishly.

"Do you think he strung you along?"

"Possibly."

"And did you know," Bob went on, "that he might go into partnership with Ken and Peter?"

"He mentioned it was in the offer."

"Do you care?"

"Not really. I'm going out on my own, everyone knows that, including Ken. He knows he's interim experience for me."

"So you don't feel bad about Sean?"

"No," Lori fibbed. She didn't want it getting around that she was dissatisfied with Sean in any way. Obviously, the way things were in the office, the gossip would get back to Sean. She needed to be guarded.

Louise came in to find her husband and Lori returned to the living room. Sean was talking to Mary and Paul. She chose a small plate and put a slice of the Black Forest cake on it. She scooped up some chocolate flakes and cream with a fork, nibbled them, and tried not to look at Sean. She didn't want to like the way he laughed, or the way his mouth looked vulnerable when he was silent, or the way his pale brown, wavy hair brushed the collar of his white sweater, or how the sweater stretched over his broad shoulders, or . . . anything. But she did like it. She liked it all.

Mary and Paul moved away from Sean and when he was alone he glanced in her direction. Quickly he came over to her.

When he reached her, he said, "You escaped from me."

"I went for coffee."

"Sounds good. Where is it?"

"In the kitchen."

Lori led the way to the kitchen and showed him where the coffeepot and the cups and saucers were. She watched him pour himself a cup. When he stood with his hips against the counter, sipping from the cup, she realized they had shared many moments like this lately, and always there was the same tension between them. But now the tension was much more familiar.

"Enjoying the party?" she asked Sean in much too bright a voice.

He gave her quizzical look. "Very much. How about you?"

"Yes. I'm enjoying it." Her fingers by her side pleated the material of her black pants. *The difference was that they weren't at work. They were in a social atmosphere. They didn't have to adhere to office rules.*

Sipping his coffee, Sean glanced around the spacious kitchen. "Nice house."

"Ken's design."

"Yes, he was telling me."

"My Dad built it."

"I met your Dad one day at the office."

Lori recalled her father had been meeting with Ken the day he had dropped Julie off.

"Is your father the reason you're an architect?"

"I suppose. I was brought up surrounded by construction."

"Interesting." Sean finished his coffee and put the cup and saucer on the counter.

Lori untwisted her fingers from the leg of her pants. "Good coffee?"

"Yes." He smiled at her. "Don't you think we're having a very strange conversation?"

"Yes."

He moved closer to her. "Let's end it."

Lori's lips seemed to beg for his kiss, and she received it: a very light touch of his mouth moving across hers; enough to set her heart racing out of control. The feelings were so intense she had to raise her hands to his chest to push him away.

"I possibly shouldn't have done that," Sean said softly as he lifted his head. "I know it's cliché, but you look so beautiful tonight."

Lori swallowed hard. She couldn't remove her gaze from the brilliance of his. His heart beat hard beneath her fingertips. She traced the ribbed pattern of his sweater with her nail.

"Did you come here in your own car tonight?" he asked huskily.

She nodded. "Yes. Why?"

He raised a hand and held her fingers still. "I was going to suggest I drive you home."

She wished she had come by taxi. She wanted to be with him.

Sean squeezed her fingers and let go of her hands. Lori moved away from him. "It's okay," she said.

He shook his head and reached out; the back of his hand gently fluttered down the side of her neck. "It's not. But drive carefully. Goodnight, Lori."

"You drive carefully as well," she told him as he moved to the kitchen door.

"I will. See you on Monday."

Lori heard his soft footsteps on the hallway tile. She heard voices. He was probably telling Caroline or Ken he was leaving. She heard a car door bang and went to the side window to watch the headlights radiate through the darkness. Sean was leaving and her heart felt it.

Lori eventually went back to join the party, but all the expectation had gone out of the evening, and when Mary and Paul decided to leave, she made her escape with the crowd. She drove home through silent cold winter streets. Once inside her house, she stared at the empty house a few doors down, the house that would soon become Sean's.

Chapter Six

On Monday Lori drove into the parking lot at the same time as Sean. They both left their vehicles together and slammed the doors.

As they walked side by side over the asphalt, Sean said softly, "Did you enjoy the party?"

Lori shifted her briefcase into her other hand and adjusted her purse on to her shoulder. She thought of his kiss. "Very much. Did you?"

"Yes. Very much."

He walked up the steps a little quicker than Lori to open the door for her. As she passed by him, Lori let herself inhale his crisp aftershave and the fresh laundered smell of his shirt. Was *he* thinking of their kiss?

Mary was at her desk watching them come in. Lori moved well away from Sean.

"Good morning, you two. George Hinton has been on the phone for either one of you. He wants a meeting pronto. He's made a decision on one of the designs."

"Thanks, Mary," Sean said. "Do you want to call him, Lori?"

She didn't expect to be invited to do that. She hid her surprise. "Well, of course I will."

"Great," Sean said. "See you later." He walked through to his office.

Lori went to her basket to gather her messages.

"You didn't come together this morning?" Mary asked.

"Heaven's no. We met in the parking lot."

"He hasn't moved in near you yet?"

"No, not for two weeks. The end of the month."

"You could carpool."

Lori shook her head. "Mary, no. I like to be independent. Besides—"

"He's not your type and you have plans, I know." Mary chuckled. "Go on and call George. He's hopping."

Lori arranged a meeting with George Hinton at three o'clock. She drove up to the ski lodge with Sean driving behind her. Elaine Hinton was in the office.

"Hi, Lori. Mr. Matheson is already in with Dad."

Lori could tell by Elaine's animated expression that she was impressed by Sean. Wasn't everyone?

Lori went through to George's boardroom. Sean smiled and beckoned her forward. It seemed that

George had approved one of Lori's favorite designs. The exterior of the lodge would be a rough stone, and the main lounge would be in the center of the building with a cathedral ceiling and a fireplace. The hotel suites would flank the lounge on two levels. This would give the lounge the appearance of a courtyard. The chalet units were left in question, however. Sean was still working on them.

"Are you pleased he chose your best design?" Sean asked, putting on his gloves as they left George's office and went out into the crisp air.

"Did you think it was my best?"

"Yes. I did."

His compliment left Lori glowing. Her footsteps felt light as she walked over to her car and got inside.

Sean honked his horn at her and waved as he left. She waved to him. She felt thrilled by his compliment, thrilled that her first major building design would grace Ashton Heights for a long time to come, thrilled that Sean hadn't overpowered her in any way. She would have expected him to want to steal the limelight.

Julie was at home preparing dinner. Lori took off her coat and went into the kitchen.

"You look as if you're dancing on the ceiling," Julie said.

Lori went to the fridge and took out a can of soda pop. "George Hinton chose my design for the new lodge and Sean didn't even question it. He didn't even make any changes. It's a go."

Julie put one hand on her hip as she stirred pasta in a pot. "That's wonderful, Lori. See, he's not the bad guy."

Lori poured the contents of the can into a glass. "I have to admit I expected more opposition. He seemed to get a handle on what I was doing and didn't interfere. So the project is still mine more or less. There are still twenty-five units to be settled, but my main ideas are a go."

"I'm really happy for you."

Lori began setting the table with cork placemats and cutlery. "Did you have a good weekend, Julie?"

"Great. How about you? Did you go out?"

"Yes. Ken had a staff party."

"Was Sean there?"

"Of course. That's who it was for really." She paused for effect. "He's bought the end house and he's moving in, in two weeks."

Julie frowned. "Which end house? Oh, on this street?"

"Naturally on this street."

"Is that good?"

"I don't know. It sort of puts him on my doorstep."

"It does. Although you never see any neighbors. I haven't seen anyone since I've been here." Julie spooned the pasta into a serving bowl. "Are you ready for dinner?"

"Definitely. I'm starved for real food."

* * *

Ken called Lori into his office the following morning. Lori sat down in the maroon leather armchair that Sean had been sitting in the first morning he arrived.

"Congratulations on George choosing your design, Lori. Sean figures you know what's going on so he's going to transfer the project entirely back to you. Alan will be coming on board with you instead."

This was new. Lori couldn't quite understand why Ken had ever put Sean on Hinton's with her if he was now letting him back off. But she wasn't going to question a decision she applauded. "That's fine," she told Ken, unsure if she wanted Sean to be off the job or not, now that she was used to working with him all the time. "What about the twenty-five units that Sean is working on?"

"We'll pass those back to you. I've been talking to George and we've discussed the possibility of moving them down the hillside on to level ground. I've got some information and I'll talk to you about it."

"Okay," Lori said. She could hardly be ungrateful now that she had got her way, but she really didn't trust the decisions that had been made. Had Sean thought they were getting too close? Had the kiss been a mistake?

"Did you enjoy the party?"

Lori glanced at Ken. "Oh, yes, very much."

"Wonderful." Ken smiled.

Lori returned Ken's smile. "Thank Caroline for me."

"I will. And by the way, your dish is in the kitchen. Your name is on the outside of the brown paper sack."

"Oh, thanks. I forgot about the salad bowl."

Lori went to the kitchen to pick up her salad bowl, then she returned to her desk. Before she sat down at her computer, she gave a silent whoop. Her project was hers again. And she enjoyed working with Alan.

Even though Julie was still staying with her, life seemed to settle down. Julie was definitely concentrating on writing a lot of songs, and when they were both in the house together working, Lori felt quite comfortable. She had probably forgotten that they were both adults now, not little girls or college students. As two adults sharing the house, they were quite companionable. And in this house, because Julie was upstairs, her guitar noise was minimal.

Lori was so busy that Sean's moving day came quickly. Even though Julie was around on Friday evening, Lori kept popping to the window to see if Sean was in the house yet. About eight o'clock she saw his wagon parked outside the garage and a light on in the kitchen.

"Is he there?"

Lori jumped around. "Julie don't scare me like that."

Julie laughed. "Do you think we should—."

"No."

"Are you just going to ignore he's living down the street?"

"Of course not, but I don't want to bother him the moment he moves in."

"Why not?"

"He'll be busy, Julie. Wait until he's settled."

"He might want some help."

"He told me this afternoon that his things aren't arriving until tomorrow morning."

"So you've discussed this with him?"

"Just casually in the office kitchen." Lori thrust her fingers into the back pockets of her jeans. The kiss in the kitchen at Ken's house had never been mentioned, but always when she was talking to Sean, she remembered it. She couldn't forget it. She relived the touch of his mouth over and over. She did plan on going over to Sean's new house, but not until after his belongings had arrived. He had told her his first night in the house would be Saturday night. He was still at the motel tonight. She hoped Julie was going out so she would be able to make up her own mind about what time to see Sean.

"Are you doing anything this weekend?" she asked.

"I'm going to Rochester tomorrow with Janine and Howard Fisher. Jake's playing hockey in a junior team."

Lori was pleased with that news. It gave her a free Saturday by herself.

Julie shrugged. "Okay. If we're not going to be

neighborly this evening, I'm going to bed early. Jan and Howard will be here at six-thirty."

In the morning, Lori waved the Fisher family and Julie goodbye, and went upstairs to dress. She was tidying the house, when she heard a roar up the street. She peered out of the window to see a big white truck blocking the entire road. Sean was outside his house in faded jeans and a thick knit sweater talking to the truck driver.

She had an idea for an unpretentious housewarming gift. She cultivated African violets. Fran had knocked down a couple recently, but Lori still had one white and one pink coming along very nicely. She went to the kitchen and sorted out the plants. Then she scooped Fran away from the counter.

Holding Fran in her arms, she watched the moving van back down the road without felling trees, denting a car or knocking bricks from the corner houses. Sean's door was now closed. He was there alone.

Lori carefully placed the plant pots into a plastic shopping bag. She wouldn't bother changing her casual appearance; her hair was in a ponytail and she wore jeans and a blue T-shirt. She wanted to appear as if she had rushed in to be, well, neighborly, as Julie felt she should have been last night. She put on her black quilted jacket, tucked her feet into sneakers, and picked up the parcel. After making sure her front door was locked, she put her key into her pocket.

Each townhouse was divided by a bank of evergreens for privacy and they lined the private road. She walked along the edge of the road to Sean's driveway and climbed the steps. Then, holding the plastic bag in one hand, she rang the doorbell.

Sean answered. Wearing only a T-shirt with his jeans now, he looked warm from exertion. "Hi, Lori. I've just been putting some of my pull-apart furniture together. Come on in."

She lifted the plastic bag. "I have some plants for you to cheer up your new house."

"Great." He stepped back to open the door wider to let her in. "I've dug out my coffeemaker and made coffee, and I was going to put together a sandwich. Want to share?"

"Sure. I would love to."

He closed the door and leaned against it, looking at her.

The hallway was like hers, narrow and a little dull. "Ken should have put in skylights," she said, looking at the ceiling instead of at Sean.

Sean glanced at the ceiling. "Great idea. Why don't we do it? We could hire the same contractor and get a deal. Like maybe your father."

He lowered his gaze and Lori couldn't help but look at him now. "My Dad would probably do it. He put one in their house last year."

"Then I think it's a great idea. We'll think about it anyway." Sean [leaned against] the door. "Go through to the kitchen."

Lori followed the smell of coffee brewing. His kitchen was reversed to hers. Also, her decor was navy blue and white, his was black and white. In keeping with the larger design of his unit, his kitchen did have a little extra space at one end, where Sean had put a round table with a mottled glass top and padded chairs. The dining set wasn't a cheap imitation either: it was heavy iron; very real.

She put her package on the table.

"Can I take your jacket?"

He strode over to her and Lori held her body taut as his hands touched her shoulders and he helped her remove her jacket. He hung her coat over the back of a kitchen chair.

"Sit down."

She sat down on the round-seated chair, placed her hands on his table, and linked her fingers together. He poured two mugs of coffee and put them down on the table, then opened the plastic bag. He took out the plants very carefully and set them gently on the counter side by side.

"Thank you, Lori. I needed these. They'll brighten the kitchen window." He carried them to the window ledge. "How's that?"

"Good. I'm glad you like them."

"I do, very much. Now, reward time. Sandwiches."

"Fine." Lori unlinked her fingers and pulled her mug closer to her.

Sean folded the plastic bag and put it with some

other's on a corner of the counter. He took a loaf, cheese and lettuce from the refrigerator.

"Dijon?" he asked, holding up a jar.

"Please."

"You seem to like the same food as me," he said, spreading on the mustard. "Black coffee, grilled cheese sandwiches, pizza." He put her plate in front of her

"Not very healthy foods," she said with a smile.

"I like salads and vegetables as well." He sat down at the table. "How about you?

"Oh, yes, me too," she said, wondering why he was comparing their likes and dislikes so closely. She had also enjoyed kissing him. If he had enjoyed kissing her, then they shared that mutual experience as well.

He lifted a half of his sandwich. "Then here's to the new house."

She lifted half of her sandwich. "I hope you'll be very content here."

He gave her a lopsided look. "I'm pleased you didn't say happy."

"Why?"

"Because content is a better word. I would rather be content for longer in life than deliriously happy in short bursts. Wouldn't you?"

"That's why I said it. Happy is transient. Content is . . . comforting." As well as food tastes, they even had the same philosophies. She wondered if that mattered to him.

He met her gaze with his. "Yes, it is comforting."
Then he glanced at the sandwich. "Who's going to
take the first bite?"

Lori glanced at her sandwich. "Why? What have
you done to it?"

"I haven't poisoned it, that's for sure. I'll go first."

After they finished eating, Sean took her on a tour
of the house. He had the same type of living room and
kitchen downstairs. On the second level was the dining
room and one of the bedrooms. Then on the top floor,
as well as the two other bedrooms, there was a big
family room that overlooked more ski hills than hers
because of the corner lot.

"I love this room," she said. "Ashton Heights looks
beautiful when you're up high."

Sean placed his hands on her shoulders. "It does,
doesn't it?"

His touch was unexpected and it made her body
tremble. He lowered his mouth to her neck and kissed
her very softly against her nape. "I like you with a
ponytail."

"I probably look twelve."

"No. Just pretty."

His hands dropped. "Anyway, this is my humble
abode."

"I like it," she said, stepping away from him.

He smiled. "Good."

They went back downstairs and Sean said, "The
house will look better when there is more furniture."

"Do you have much more?"

"A few choice items."

"Minimalist?"

He chuckled. "You could say that. How about you?"

"Minimalist to the extreme."

Lori picked up her jacket at the door. She didn't want to overstay her welcome.

Sean walked her down the road to her house. "Thanks for the plants, Lori. It was sweet of you. Have you told Julie I'm nearly next door?"

"Yes, I have. She's in Rochester for most of the day."

"If she comes home in good time, just tell her to drop on over."

"Okay. I will." He wasn't inviting her again she noticed. She would really like to know what his kisses were all about. Or did he just take advantage of random moments to kiss her?

"See you then, Lori," he said and loped back to his house.

Lori shopped during the afternoon and went home to a quiet house. She was actually glad Fran was with her; she chatted to the cat as she fed her and while Fran followed her around.

Julie wasn't as late as Lori had thought she would be. She left the Fisher's minivan and hurried inside with a mock-shiver. "Brrr, it's getting cold out there." She unzipped her silver leather jacket.

"How was the hockey game?"

"Fine, but the Ashton Bullets didn't win. Did Sean get moved in?"

"Yes. He's in." Lori stood in the shadows, still holding Fran. "He's invited you over."

"Then you've been over already?"

"I just took him some plants and had lunch with him."

"Just had lunch." Julie laughed. "Lori, you're understating your relationship with him."

No, she wasn't. He had given her lunch because she had brought him plants. He hadn't tried to stop her leaving when she did, and he had told her to send Julie over. He didn't invite her again.

Julie frowned. "Lori, I can tell you're nuts about the guy. So grab your coat. We'll go before we have dinner."

"You go alone," Lori said. Fran wriggled around and she let the cat go. Fran stretched and looked at her as if she too was saying, *Go and see Sean.*

Julie sighed deeply and zipped her jacket. "All right. I'll go alone. See you later."

Lori went to the window and watched Julie walk over to Sean's house under the streetlights. Sean's wagon wasn't in the driveway. He had either put his wagon into his garage or he was out. Lori hoped he was out. That meant Julie would come back again. She pressed her fist against the window. She wasn't going to enjoy having Sean so close. She was in danger of spying on everything that went on at his house.

Julie reached Sean's door. She knocked. The door opened and Sean appeared. Julie went inside and the door closed.

As Lori kept watch on the house, a sleek car purred up the private road. Lori watched the car slip into Sean's driveway. A woman stepped out. She wore high-heeled boots, a pair of slacks and a short dressy coat. Her hair was pale and long, and blew in the breeze as she walked up the steps.

The door opened immediately and Sean embraced the woman and invited her into his house. The door closed. Now that woman and Julie were in the house with Sean.

Fran rubbed around her legs.

"Oh, Franny," she said forlornly.

Lori carried Fran upstairs to her office. The cat curled in a ball on an old sweater Lori had tossed in one corner, and Lori turned on her computer to try and work. But all she did was stare at the screen and ended up playing Solitaire again. She had one ear on the front door, hoping it might open so Julie would come home. Julie, at least, would tell her who Sean's friend was.

When the phone rang, she was pleased for the distraction. She hoped it was her mother or Susan so she could have a long chat.

"Lori, it's Sean."

"Hi," she said stiffly.

"Julie's over here as you probably know, and I have someone here I would like you to meet."

He had some nerve if he wanted her to meet a girl-friend. No way. She didn't want to meet her. "I'm busy working on Hinton's right now, Sean."

"On a Saturday night?"

"It doesn't matter what night it is for me to work."

"Obviously not. Aren't you worried about becoming a workaholic?"

"I probably am one already."

"Then take a break. Come on over. I did invite you to come with Julie."

"No, you didn't."

"I thought it was obvious."

"It wasn't."

"I'm sorry then. Please come over now. I want you to meet my mother."

"Your mother?"

"She's here for dinner and I'm going to invite both you and Julie to join us."

Suddenly life seemed right again. Lori felt like jumping up and down with delight. "All right. I'll be there in about twenty minutes."

"Great. Thanks, Lori."

Even though she knew that Julie had gone to Sean's wearing jeans, Lori changed her clothes. She put on black slacks and a pearl gray sweater. Wearing her black coat, she walked beneath the streetlights to his house.

Sean came to answer the door. "Hey," he said, drawing her in with his hand on her arm. "This is my mother, Barbara Matheson."

Barbara's hair was a silvery color; possibly gray with a color rinse. She was very slim and sophisticated in a pair of burgundy slacks and a matching silk blouse and gold jewelry.

"I'm really pleased to meet you, Lori. Sean told me he was working with a woman architect. I thought that was nice."

Lori shook hands with Barbara, wondering if that was what Sean thought as well. "It's my pleasure to meet you."

Lori took off her coat and Sean hung it up for her. Then she glanced at Julie, who gave her an I-told-you-so smirk.

Sean led the way upstairs to the dining room, and while Sean and Barbara returned downstairs to deal with the dinner, Julie lounged in a fabric armchair. "I told you, you should have come over with me."

Lori sat down on a black leather office style chair. "Did you suggest I come?"

Julie patted her hair. "No. I didn't say a word. When I arrived he showed me around the house. He asked, "Where's Lori?" I said, "At home. She told me she'd seen the house already." He looked a little disappointed at that. Anyway, a little while later his mother arrived for dinner, and he suggested—as they had made oodles of noodles, or in real terms, lasagna—that he would invite you over to eat with us."

"So here I am," Lori said, glancing around. Sean had placed one abstract oil painting on the wall, but that was about the extent of his decor. Some unopened boxes sat in one corner. "Earlier on, he invited you, Julie, but he didn't invite me, so I didn't think I was welcome."

"You're so touchy about him that I'm positive you're in love with him."

Lori made a face at her sister, willing her to keep quiet, as Barbara came upstairs with a tray. Julie and Lori stood up to help her set the dining room table. As soon as it was ready they all sat around the square wood-block table on high-backed chairs with comfortable padded seats.

"It's nice for me to have Sean close by again," Barbara said. "His father died just over a year ago and I was feeling a little lonely with both my children away."

"Does your daughter visit?" Lori asked.

"Not too often. She has two school-age children. Mostly I go to her in D.C. when she needs some babysitting done."

"Then it's lucky Sean could find a job closer to you."

"It is lucky. Although I was on him to open his own business, he said he wasn't quite ready for that yet."

"He seems to be ready for a partnership with Randall & Rhodes, though," Lori said.

"He's mentioned that, but it's a long way off I think. How long have you been with the firm?"

"I've been with Ken on and off for years, since I was a teenager. I worked for him during college. Then he joined forces with Peter Rhodes, and now I've been full-time for two years."

"And you like working for him?"

"Yes. Very much."

"Sean says it's quite a casual atmosphere. Less so than his city job, which was in one of those large offices."

"Yes, it's casual in some respects," Lori said. "But we have to work hard."

"He's mentioned that as well."

Sean came in with the food and sat down at the table with the women.

The lasagna was spicy and tasty, and the salad was crisp. Julie kept a conversation going with some stories about her musical gigs in strange bars. Then they turned the discussion to art.

"Do you two ever come to the ice sculpture festival in Ellis Corners?" Barbara asked.

"I went last February," Lori said. "Didn't you used to go a lot, Julie?"

Julie nodded. "Yes. I had a boyfriend who was a sculptor and used to enter the show."

"I thought so."

Barbara smiled. "In that case, you might both be interested. It starts tomorrow. Sean is coming in to take me around. Why don't you two come with him?"

Sean glanced at both Julie and Lori. "Do you want to? I'm game."

"I'm busy tomorrow," Julie said. "But Lori would like to go, I'm sure."

She did feel backed up against a wall this evening. However, if she went out with Sean on the weekend it would be like a test. She might find that familiarity bred contempt, or whatever the saying was. She really did want to move Sean down to a level where she could feel absolutely normal in his presence. And then there was the thought of another Sunday alone. She had never felt the tiniest bit lonely until she met Sean.

"All right," she said quickly before she could think up excuses as to why she shouldn't go. "I would like that."

"Then you're invited to dinner at my house after the festival," Barbara told her. "Are you sure you can't come Julie?"

"I've made plans. Thank you, though."

Barbara left not long after dinner and Sean walked Julie and Lori home.

"See you tomorrow," he said to Lori at the door. "About ten."

"Fine," she said.

Julie whooped when they were inside Lori's house. "You have a date."

Lori hung up her coat. "It's not really a date."

Julie tossed her jacket on the bench. "What would you call it then?"

Lori narrowed her eyes at her sister. "Probably something maneuvered by you."

"I didn't maneuver that. Barbara asked clear out of the blue."

"Maybe, but Sean couldn't get out of it, could he?"

"And you think he really wants to?"

Lori sighed. "How do I know what he wants?"

"You'll find out when you date him, Lori. That's the way you discover if you are in love with him. It's silly to be mooning around over a man. You have to confront your feelings."

"Except I don't want to be in love right now. However, I do know I should confront my feelings. That's why I'm going with him."

"Good. Relax and take life as it comes."

"I've been taking life as it comes ever since Sean started at Ken's office, and it's driving me crazy. But I've got to get some order back in my life. I feel as if I'm out of control."

"I know what you mean, Lori. That's why I left L.A. Honestly, I'm not trying to push you two together. It would be kind of sweet, but if it's not going to happen, it won't. I've had tons of boyfriends who are just friends, Lori. You can't stop dating just because you've planned your career in one direction."

"I suppose that's true."

"Listen to me. I'm your older sister. I've been where you are. You have to figure out what is most important in your life."

"I know what's important," Lori said. "My architectural career."

"Then you've made your decision. You stick to it. It's that simple."

Maybe it was simple for Julie, Lori thought as she got ready for bed. For her, it was complex. And she didn't think she *had* made her decision. She was far too excited about seeing Sean tomorrow for any decision to have been made.

Chapter Seven

By the time Lori put on her quilted jacket and a warm scarf, her excitement had quelled slightly about the trip to see the ice sculptures. She pushed her feet into warm leather boots as Julie came downstairs wearing a nightshirt.

Julie leaned over the banister. "Looking forward to it?"

Lori tugged her scarf more firmly around her neck. "I don't know. I have misgivings."

"So your decision wasn't final?"

"Yes, it was final."

"Then, no problem."

"No. No problem." Lori waved her gloved hand. "Anyway, see you later. Have a good day."

"You too."

Lori left the house. She saw Sean brushing the snow from his wagon. When she reached his driveway he turned around.

"Hi," he said. "Cold, isn't it?"

The air held that sort of damp cold that crept into the bones. "It is." Lori glanced up at the gray swollen sky. "Do you think it's going to snow all day?"

"According to my mother, it isn't snowing in Ellis Corners, so this might be local. But it does appear to be moving in that direction—straight east."

"Really, for ice sculpture you need bright sun." Was she trying to weasel out of this trip? Didn't she have the guts to face her feelings? Or even the guts to find out what her actual feelings were? This outing might be all she needed to cure her of Sean. And what about him? What was he going to get out of this? Was he just going along with his mother's whim?

Sean stopped brushing snow. "I guess it would be nice if the sun shone, but at least it's cold enough for the ice not to melt."

Lori pushed her gloved hands deep into her jacket pockets. "I suppose." She *would* go through with this.

Sean tossed the brush into the back. "Are you ready?"

"Yes." Lori climbed into his warm wagon.

The ride to Ellis Corners was on a two-lane high-way. Lori had never driven the distance with another architect beside her, someone who saw the same building detail she did. They both noticed interesting houses, or commercial holdings.

"That is an ugly peaked roof on that school," Sean said as they entered the town limits.

Lori laughed. "Isn't that Ellis High?"

"Oh, yeah." He grinned. "I thought it was an ugly roof then, as well. I remember redesigning it when I was a teenager."

"Did you always want to be an architect?"

"Always," he said. "My Dad was an engineer. I suppose there is a correlation there."

"Does your mother work?"

"She used to work with Dad. When he died, she sold the company for a tidy profit. She works part-time at a friend's store, and I think she's perfectly content doing that."

Ellis Corners was smaller than Ashton Heights but the setting was on a pretty lake which kept the tourists coming in the summer. One small ski resort nearby also filled the motels in winter. The surrounding countryside was spotted with horse and market farms, and Lori knew the area was a great place to go berry-picking.

Sean drove through some residential streets until he came to a street of identical small white-sided bungalows—probably condos. He parked in one of the driveways.

"Did you live here when you were a kid?" Lori asked, as they walked to the front door.

"No. Mom and Dad bought this a few years ago, hoping they could retire in it, but Dad didn't make it long enough to retire."

Lori saw him try to smile, but he didn't do a very good job.

Barbara opened the door before they had a chance to ring the doorbell.

"Come on in. It's cold but it looks brighter than it did earlier. Did you have much snow your way?"

"Just a little," Lori told her.

"That's good. I heard there was snow in the forecast. I'll just get my things. Go through to the kitchen and help yourself to coffee if you want."

Lori liked the compact bungalow; it was like her parents' home before her father done all the renovations. She hoped her parents would both be around to enjoy retirement.

Sean poured himself some coffee. Lori shook her head; she didn't want anymore. She was drinking far too much coffee since Sean's arrival in her life.

In her life? Was that how she saw his presence here?

She watched him sipping coffee. He wore his leather jacket over a black turtleneck sweater. His hair always looked brighter and lighter when he wore black. He didn't speak, he merely returned her gaze.

Lori clasped her hands loosely in her lap.

"Something the matter?" he asked.

She shook her head. "No. Why?"

He grinned. "Oh, you seem very somber."

His white smile mesmerized her. "I've been thinking."

"It's Sunday. A day off. Don't think. Enjoy."

The doorbell rang. Lori heard Barbara go to answer it.

Sean frowned.

"You look somber now," Lori said.

"I've just figured something out."

Barbara bustled in, wearing an emerald green parka over the same shade of slacks and sweater. Following her was a man, probably in his late fifties, stocky like Ken Randall, but with gray hair. He wore jeans and a bulky blue padded jacket.

"This is Mike MacDonald. My son, Sean, and an architect he works with in Ashton Heights, Lori Fenton. Mike has recently moved in next door and I thought it would be nice for him to come with us." Barbara sounded extremely breathless.

Mike moved briskly forward and extended his hand. "I'm pleased to meet you, Sean. I've heard a lot about you, naturally. And Lori, it's a pleasure to meet you as well." He shook hands with both of them.

Lori glanced at Sean's expression as Mike stepped back to be beside his mother. He didn't look too happy.

"Anyway," Barbara said. "We're ready. Let's go."

They drove to the ice festival in Sean's vehicle. Barbara and Mike sat in the rear. A stilted conversation went back and forth. Lori explained her career. Mike explained he had retired from engineering. Sean said little. He concentrated on the traffic which was quite heavy. People came from afar to see what artists and sculptors from all around the world could create from blocks of ice.

After Sean had parked, they walked to the exhibition. Barbara suggested they split up.

"We'll meet back at the hotdog stand in a couple of hours," she told Sean. "All right?"

His gaze was steady on his mother's face. "Yep. Fine."

As the other couple walked away, Mike's gloved hand moving for Barbara's, Lori said, "You didn't know about him?"

Sean swallowed hard. "I knew about him. I hadn't met him yet, and I didn't know he was coming with us today."

"Is it serious?"

"I suppose. She seems to like him quite a bit."

"I would say she likes him a lot. Didn't you like him?"

"Liking him isn't the point. It's just strange seeing my mother with a man other than my father. I saw my father about a year before he died, and then when he had his heart attack, I couldn't get home quick enough. There was a snowstorm and I got stranded at the airport overnight. By the time I finally got here, he was gone."

Lori automatically reached for his hand and squeezed through their gloves. "I'm sorry."

She expected Sean to pull his hand away from hers, but he didn't. They began walking, holding hands, the way Mike and Barbara had.

"I suppose I should be more generous," Sean said. "Mother deserves happiness."

"She's still young and attractive."

"I realize that."

"It might not come to anything. Is this her first relationship since your dad died?"

"As far as I know."

"It's not why you came back to be closer to her?"

"Not because of Mike. I didn't know about Mike until I came back here. She just mentioned she had dated her next door neighbor a few times lately. I didn't know today was going to be the official introduction."

"Well, it was," Lori said cheerfully. "I really don't think you can interfere. She's a grown woman."

Sean semi-smiled at her. "Do you think they're in love?"

"I don't know much about love."

"No?"

She shook her head. "It's something I've avoided. I'm waiting until I'm settled in my own firm."

"You have someone marked for this?"

"What do you mean?"

"I mean, do you have someone who is willing to wait until you're ready?"

"No."

"What if you don't find anyone?"

She shrugged. "I guess I don't."

"You have to be careful, Lori," he said softly. "I found someone once, but I wasn't ready for what we were feeling, so I let her go. It doesn't work. I ached for her for a long time."

Lori felt his fingers tighten on hers. "Do you still ache?" she asked.

"No, I got over it."

"But you never met anyone else?"

"No. Not yet."

Which ruled her out, Lori decided.

"But if I do meet someone," Sean continued. "I'll go for it. No waiting this time. So I suppose I shouldn't get on mother for having a boyfriend after all."

Lori shook her head. "Not if you have the philosophy that you should go for what you have and not wait."

"I just believe you can't plan your life. Look at my dad, for instance. All his life he made plans for when he would be free of his business and he never was free. Never."

Lori squeezed his hand some more. "Then be generous to your mother. Let her have some fun."

"I suppose I should. I wonder if today was really

the day she was going to introduce me to Mike, or if she figured having you here would soften the blow and keep me off her back." He smiled crookedly at her.

Lori stopped walking. They stood apart, but still holding hands. "You mean, I've been used?"

"I didn't mean that, Lori. I'm sorry. I wanted you to come with us, but I just think that your presence has made the news easier for me to digest. If I had been alone with Mike and Mom, I would have fumed all day. In other words, you've helped me see that I would have behaved like a spoiled brat son."

Lori chuckled, and at the same time felt a shift in their relationship. They had moved to one more stage: intimate revelations.

Sean pulled her by the hand. "Come closer."

Lori moved closer to him. Today she wouldn't question their relationship. So she let him kiss her gently with ice-cold lips.

She moved her head abruptly away. "Ooh."

He grinned. "Cold?"

"Freezing."

"Then let's walk and see what we've come to see."

It was easy to not think about her personal life when she was admiring the beautifully carved crystal-like castles and figures. She discovered, she shared with Sean, a similar eye for design. They liked the same shapes. It was their philosophies that were different: Lori liked to plan; Sean liked to go for the moment.

After they had seen most of the exhibition they went

to the hotdog stand to meet Barbara and Mike. As they approached the older couple, Lori noticed that they were glancing at one another with intimate gazes. She figured that this relationship with Mike was important to Barbara, and that gaining Sean's approval was crucial.

While they all sat at a small table, drinking cider and munching on hot dogs, the snow began—big fluffy flakes that quickly accumulated and placed an extra glitter on the sculptures.

The white stuff was coming down hard and fast on the return trip to Barbara's bungalow. Sean parked in the driveway and Mike helped him shovel out the pathway. Sean then went over to help Mike do his path. Lori saw Sean's move as a move of goodwill to get to know Mike for his mother's sake.

"I hope Sean likes Mike," Barbara said to Lori. They were in the kitchen and Barbara was heating a casserole she had prepared earlier. "Did he say anything to you?"

Lori placed some paper napkins on a tray. They were going to eat in the other room by the fire, which Sean had yet to start. "I could tell he was surprised, let's say, but we discussed the situation and I think he came to terms with it. He told me about his father."

Holding an oven mitt, Barbara said, "That's half of his problem; he didn't get home in time to see his dad again and he feels that he hasn't closed that segment of his life . . . which I have. I tried to explain that to him when I told him about Mike. I hope you didn't mind coming along and being in the middle of it?"

"Was that the intention?" Lori asked.

"It helped, let's say. I also saw that Sean was interested in you and knew it wouldn't be a hardship for him to have you along."

"This entire area of New York loves to match-make," Lori said.

"Well, we have long snowy winters. Men are handy for shoveling snow."

Lori laughed. "Sean's definitely inherited the snow-clearing gene, but I don't want to get involved in a serious relationship. Casual dates are the best."

Barbara sighed. "Oh, dear. Then you don't find my son devastatingly attractive?"

Lori couldn't fib. The words flowed easily. "Oh, yes."

"He can't keep his eyes off you, Lori."

Lori was about to protest, but Sean came in rubbing his hands. "It's cold. Mike's not staying, Mom?"

"No, his daughter is next door with the kids."

"Okay. The dinner smells good. I'll go fix the fire."

Sean lit a log fire in the fireplace. Lori tried to relax on the chintz sofa with a cup of hot chocolate, but she kept looking outside the window. The wind was blowing and the snow was piling up. Sean's vehicle was covered. The path he had shoveled was already blown in. Snowstorms always made her uneasy, and the drive home would be treacherous.

They ate supper sitting around the blazing fire.

"I was thinking," Barbara said, as she came back from the kitchen with some dessert. "Do you guys want to stay overnight? The weather out there is not improving."

"We'll be okay," Sean said.

"Go out and take a look," his mother said. "And check the road report on the radio."

Lori looked at Barbara as Sean got up to leave them. "We have to be at work tomorrow."

"It might be safer to drive early in the morning."

"Possibly." But Lori was fidgety. She didn't want anyone to know in the office that she had stayed overnight at Sean's mother's house. She didn't think there would be disapproval on anyone's part if she did date Sean, but she didn't feel comfortable with the reputation that might follow.

Sean returned. "It's really bad. I found a radio report and the highway to Ashton Heights is down to single lane traffic. They're advising motorists to stay off the roads. It's supposed to blow through overnight. Do you want to stay, Lori?" He sat down and picked up his plate of cake.

"Do I have a choice?" she asked.

He shook his head. "Not really. I don't think it's worth risking the trip, when we can do it safer in a few hours."

"I would feel better if you stayed, Lori," Barbara said.

"I have to phone my sister to let her know," Lori said.

"Go ahead. There's a phone in the dining room. It's private."

Lori went to the dining room and found the telephone on a small side table. She sat down on one of the dining room chairs and punched her home number. She supposed she was hoping to get her answering machine, but instead Julie answered.

"How's the snow there?" Lori asked.

"Thick. Are you at Barbara's?"

"Yes, I am. I thought you were going out today."

"Plans were canceled."

Lori was dubious that Julie had actually had plans today. Julie wasn't beyond matchmaking either.

"So what's happening? Did you have a good time?"

"Yes. It was quite nice. But we're snowed in, so I'll be home in the morning."

"Fine. I'm glad you're safe. See you tomorrow."

"Thanks, Julie." Lori hung up the phone and returned to the other room.

Sean glanced at her as she sat down in an armchair. "Was Julie at your place?"

"Yes. She's home."

"So she knows you're safe. That's good." Barbara smiled. "Now that it's all settled, I'll go and fix up the spare bedroom for Lori. Sean will stay in his room in the basement."

Staying at Barbara's wasn't as uncomfortable as

Lori had at first feared. She was given a small guest room at the back of the bungalow with an adjoining bathroom where she felt extremely private.

A knock on the door in the morning woke her up. She quickly realized where she was and scrambled for her watch. Six-thirty.

"Lori, it's Sean. Are you awake?"

"Yes." She brushed her hair from her eyes and called out. "I'll get up now. Thanks for waking me up."

"Oh, you're welcome. I know you could probably sleep through until midday."

"How did you get up?"

"Mom woke me."

Lori laughed. "See, you're no better than me."

"I know that. We have lots of similarities. Anyway, coffee's on in the kitchen."

"Thank you."

Lori lay back on the pillow for a little longer, thinking about those similarities, then she reluctantly removed herself from the comfortable bed for her shower. Wearing the same clothes as the day before felt strange, but as she walked into the kitchen, where Sean and his mother were sitting at the table chatting, she noticed Sean was dressed in the same clothes, too.

Sean smiled at her. "Apparently, the road will soon be open. So as soon as we've dug our way out here, we can leave." He rose from his chair. "I'll get shoveling."

Barbara served her toast, orange juice, and coffee, then Lori went outside to help Sean.

His face was red with cold and exertion. "You don't have to help."

"Sure I do." She went to pick up another shovel leaning against the step. "I want to get to work on time."

"It's already a quarter to eight," he told her.

"Then we won't make it."

"We'll think up some excuse. How about an early site meeting?"

"That might go over."

"We'll try it anyway."

With two working it didn't take too long to get the short driveway cleared and his vehicle ready to leave.

Lori hoped they might make a rapid trip, but there was still snow-clearing machinery on the roads, and a brisk wind made the highway slippery.

As they moved closer to the city, Sean punched his cell phone.

He told Mary they would both be in around ten o'clock.

"We had an early meeting," he added to Mary, glancing at Lori and winking. "So we decided not to come in first thing and just met on site."

Lori hoped Mary would believe that story.

Sean disconnected his mobile phone. "It'll be okay," he said.

"I don't want to be the center of gossip."

"You won't be, Lori. No one will care."

But she did, she thought as they entered the outskirts of Ashton Heights at 9:25.

Naturally, Julie had to be home while Lori quickly changed into a long skirted suit for work.

"Don't say a word," she warned her sister, who stood by her bedroom door watching her brush her hair. "It was strictly an emergency stay-over and I hardly saw Sean."

"I'm not saying a word. I'm just watching you."

Lori put down her brush and picked up her purse from a chair. "Why are you watching me?"

"I'm noticing that you've changed since I arrived."

"I haven't changed, Julie. But I am trying to stay focused."

"Focused on Sean."

"No." She slung the strap over her shoulder. "I'm ready to leave now anyway."

Julie stood with Fran in her arms and waved Lori goodbye.

Lori couldn't drive fast because some of the roads were still clogged with snow, but she felt like driving fast; she wished it were summer, so she could just take off for a day or two alone. She needed some time to think. The weather this morning was too much like the Monday morning when she had met Sean for the first time.

Sean had already arrived. His vehicle was neatly parked in line with the others. At least they weren't arriving together, Lori thought as she pushed open the front door.

Luckily, it was Jennifer on the reception desk and she was talking on the phone. Lori hustled past her and went to her office. She turned on her computer as she took off her coat. She wanted it to appear as if she had been here for hours. But as the day passed, and no one said a word about her late arrival, she supposed that everyone had believed Sean's cell phone call about the early site meeting.

Sean came by on his way out to lunch. "Settling down?" he asked.

"Yes," she told him. "I think the meeting was believable."

"Seems that way." He smiled. "Don't be so serious, Lori. Take life as it comes."

"Our philosophies really differ."

"Possibly. Now, I'm going for lunch. I'll see you later."

Lori didn't see him later. And as the week continued, Lori began to think that Sean's arrival had been a mere flurry, a blip on her calendar, nothing more. A calm had suddenly come over her life, and it continued into the next week. She had space to work. And work she did—long hours on Hinton's Ski Lodge until she began to see her design for the Lodge flourish into a viable building. Sometimes she couldn't quite believe that Sean hadn't made this *his* job. Apparently, he was working on something else.

Lori was pleased with this outcome. All her premonitions of Sean taking over her position hadn't come to fruition. She was in charge and in control. She saw Sean in passing in the office, much as she saw any other member of the staff, and she hadn't had any contact with him at home. She was pleased about this. And Julie would soon be leaving. She had purchased a white minivan and was going to use it to travel to New York City. Life had settled down. She had made a mountain out of a molehill, as her mother had always told her she did. She was going to have to learn to not be dramatic and overstate situations.

Everything was fine.

Chapter Eight

Lori took a load of work home with her for the weekend. Julie would probably be out, seeing as it was Friday night, and Fran would be the only company she would have. She was getting used to having the little cat around now. She didn't even mind serving meals and litter box duty. Fran was becoming her companion.

Julie *was* out. There was a note on the kitchen table saying she would be back late.

"Hey, we're going to have a good time this evening," Lori said to Fran, as she stripped off her coat and eased her feet from her boots. "We have the whole house to ourselves."

Lori changed into leggings and a long sweater. She fed Fran, took her work upstairs to her computer, and prepared it for the next morning. This evening, she decided, she would have a bubble bath, watch television for a while and have something to eat, then go to bed early, so she would be fresh to work tomorrow.

She was just about to go into the bathroom when the phone rang. She went and answered it in case it was her mother.

"Lori? This is Janine Fisher."

"Hi, Janine. How are you? Julie isn't in this evening. She said she would be back late, but I'll leave her—"

"No, it's fine, Lori. It's you I want to talk to. I'm having a surprise party for Julie next Saturday. She's leaving a week Monday, you know."

Lori didn't know exactly. But she supposed she did now.

"Anyway, Lori, I was wondering if you could get her over to my house that Saturday evening. I've got the perfect excuse."

"Which is?"

"Howard and I want a sun room extension on the house. Can you help us? I know you did your father's. I love it."

"Sure, I can help you," Lori said. "But how does that get Julie to your house?"

"Well, you're working with Sean Matheson, I understand. He played ball with Howard at Ellis. I thought both you and Sean could make the excuse you're coming to my place to make plans for the sun room, and bring Julie along with you."

Lori sighed. She felt Sean was all sorted out. She didn't want to get involved with him outside of work again. "Julie's very busy, Jan. She might have other plans."

"Don't let her make other plans. Tell her I called and that I want the sun room and she's to come over with you and Sean as it's her last weekend in town."

"All right, Janine. I'll see what I can do." Lori could only hope Julie did have plans.

"Great. Let me know. Here's my phone number."

Lori wrote down Janine's number, hung up, and returned to the bathroom. She was bent over the bath, her hand on the tap, when the doorbell buzzed. She went to look out of the window that gave her a good view of the front. Sean was standing on her path.

So much for her peaceful evening. Lori dashed down the stairs and opened the door. "Hi," she said, trying for a little impatience in her voice, a terse inflection that might make him realize he was interrupting her evening. Except, she didn't need to try for a breathless voice. Her heart immediately began beating much too fast when she saw him in jeans, black sweatshirt, and sneakers. She thought she had overcome this infatuation.

"Hi, Lori," he said with a smile. "Do you have a vacuum cleaner I could borrow?"

"Yes. Don't you have one?"

"I do, but I think it needs a new belt or something. I've got friends coming for dinner in about an hour and I don't have time to take it apart, go buy parts, and then clean the place, so may I borrow yours?"

"Sure." Lori went to the closet, opened the door and tugged out the vacuum cleaner.

Sean stood behind her to help her.

"Thanks," she told him. Everything wasn't fine. She wasn't over him. She could feel his presence like a beating pulse.

"Thank you. I'll bring it back shortly."

After the door had closed, Lori sighed. Now she couldn't have her bath until Sean returned with the vacuum cleaner. She decided to watch TV while she waited, but as soon as she had settled down in a chair with the remote control, the phone rang. She reached for her cordless, which was close to the sofa.

"Hi, Lori, it's Sean. Do you have any attachments for this vacuum cleaner?"

"Aren't they attached to the handle?"

"No. They aren't."

"Julie's been cleaning. Maybe she took them off. I'll look and bring them over."

"Thanks. Sorry to bother you."

Lori went to the closet and found the attachments had been tossed into a basket. She popped them into a plastic grocery bag, grabbed her key, and a jacket, pushed her feet into hiking boots, which she felt didn't look at all glamorous with leggings, and trudged over to Sean's.

He was at the door to greet her. "You're a good kid, Lori. I'll just be a moment, then I'll carry everything back to your place."

"Do you want me to wait?" She might as well.

"If you don't mind. I'm cooking a meal for a couple of friends I went to college with. They're married and on their way to Buffalo to see Amber's parents, so they're dropping in here on the way for dinner, to catch up on old times, and they're staying the night as well. They're both architects. Would you like to have dinner and meet them?"

Lori wanted her bath. She didn't want an evening with Sean.

When she didn't answer right away, Sean said, "Please. It would be nice to have four people at dinner, instead of three. Look, I'll go finish this cleaning and you can make up your mind. Go through to the kitchen. Help yourself to potato chips and a soft drink if you like."

Lori went through to the kitchen. The room was warm from a meal cooking in the oven. She wondered what type of thing Sean cooked. Her father had never cooked. Her mother handled that side of the home.

She peered into the oven and saw a browned roasted chicken. Her stomach rumbled with hunger. She should have eaten earlier, so she wouldn't feel so hungry. Now she was tempted to stay. It might also be an interesting experience to meet some of Sean's friends, to see what type of people were attracted to him. It would also be interesting to meet another woman architect.

She didn't pour herself a drink from the cans set out on a tray, but she did nibble on some of the potato chips. Eventually, she heard the vacuum cleaner noise stop. She walked into the hallway as he came down the stairs with the cleaner. All the attachments were now neatly in place along the handle.

"What have you decided?"

She had to work with him. If she did anything to upset him, he could make her working life less agreeable. After all, he had been more than generous, keeping her on the Hinton job. He could have bullied his way in and taken over. And she was hungry.

"All right," she said. "Thank you very much. I'll go back and change clothes."

His gaze moved from her hiking boots to her tousled hair. "You look great."

"Not for meeting your friends."

"They're old friends, Lori. It'll be a casual evening. I'm staying in jeans."

She eyed her bulky hiking boots. "Different footwear then."

"All right." He smiled.

Sean carried the vacuum cleaner back to her house. "You being there will also keep Amber and Justin off my back. Just because they're married, they're pressuring me."

"But you don't have anyone to marry." *She said, hopefully.*

"No, I don't. But, unlike you, I rather yearn for some stability on the home front."

"Not many men admit that."

"Probably not, but I'm admitting it." He grinned.

His smile undid her. A few days of distance from him and she had put her feelings back in a neat package. Since she was last with him at the ice sculpture exhibit, she had felt as if she had taped up her heart. But as she walked up the driveway of her home, her emotions seemed to come cascading out of nowhere, flooding her.

She dug in her jacket pocket for her key and opened her front door so that he could carry in her vacuum cleaner.

Sean parked her vacuum cleaner in her closet, closed the door and turned around. Lori just stood there looking at him. She knew what was going to happen before it did. Sean placed his hand on the wall and bent his head. His lips met hers, very softly at first, tantalizing.

Leaving her feeling weak, he raised his head. "What if it happened?"

"It?"

"You fell in love before your allotted time. Or a

man fell in love with you and wouldn't wait. Would you change the design of your life?"

She had made her decision. She had set her goals. Just because Sean's kiss tingled on her lips was no reason for her to sway from those goals.

Before she could answer, he kissed her again. Lori couldn't stop her response. As his arms moved around her, padded jacket and all, she wrapped her own arms around his neck. She hadn't realized how badly she had wanted to run her fingers through the thick hair at the back of his neck, or how she needed to feel his mouth move over hers. His heart beat hard through his sweatshirt. Her heart pounded in her ears. As someone during the past few weeks had said, "Love is urgent."

It was Sean who ended their kiss. *One of them had to*, Lori thought as he pressed into the shadows so she couldn't quite see his expression. She had no will-power. None at all. She was disappointed by her lack of strength.

"See you at my place for dinner in about an hour, then," he said quite brusquely.

She didn't answer him. She merely stood and watched him let himself out of her front door. She slipped off her jacket and tossed it on the bench. She heard it slip to the floor, but she couldn't think about it. As it was, she could barely make her way to her bedroom.

She slumped down on the bed.

She buried her face in her hands.

She knew he wouldn't wait.

Lori managed to blank the kiss from her mind enough to concentrate on her appearance this evening. She changed the old sweatshirt for a long dusky pink velvet knit top, but left on the black leggings. She brushed her hair and clipped it casually on her head, pulling down wisps beside her ears. She was dressing for Sean; she knew that. She slipped flat black shoes on her feet.

There was a small black BMW in the driveway when she got there. Sean opened the door to her knock. He still wore his jeans but with a black shirt. She could smell he was freshly shaved.

"Hi." He didn't smile.

His bland expression knocked the wind out of her as if she had been punched in the stomach. She said, "Hi," in what she hoped was a brusque tone.

Lori heard voices upstairs as he let her in and closed the door. He took her coat from her, hung it in the closet on a hanger, then took her hand. "Come on up."

Lori was surprised that after the non-smile he wanted to hold hands with her. She went with him up the stairs, connected to him by his warm fingers folded around hers. *Love is urgent.*

In the chairs she and Julie had lounged in not long ago were a couple dressed in black: black jeans, black sweaters, short black hair.

"Amber and Justin Thomas," Sean introduced to Lori. "I'll get us drinks."

While Sean was gone Lori found out that Amber and Justin ran their own architectural firm in New York.

"We went out on our own as soon as we were engaged," Amber told Lori. "That was four years ago. Now that we're married it's no different."

"And it works?"

"Definitely." Amber smiled. "It's great being together all day."

"You don't have professional differences?"

"Naturally, but we compromise."

Sean arrived with drinks and they talked some more. It was obvious to Lori that Sean, Amber, and Justin were good friends, but they still included Lori.

As they began to eat dinner, Amber asked, "Are you interested in working with Sean?"

Interested? Was she interested? No, she wasn't interested. She wanted to open her own business by herself. She still had that goal. Just because a man had kissed her as if there were no tomorrow didn't mean she would give up her ambition. "Heavens, no. Sean has possibilities in the firm we're in at the moment. I don't. In about two years I'll open my own company. I want to be Ashton Heights' first woman architect."

Amber's smooth forehead creased. "Aren't you that already?"

"What?"

"Ashton Heights' first woman architect."

Lori had never thought about that. "I suppose I am,"

she said with a small laugh. "I didn't think of it that way. I thought I should have my name posted on a sign first."

"That's nice, but there is a lot of responsibility that goes with being on your own. I have Justin for support, but you would have to deal with staff and all the problems on your own."

"Do you have staff?"

"We employ one architectural technician full-time, and one on a part-time basis. That's all we can afford for now."

"I know the pitfalls, but I still intend to go out on my own."

"You have so much determination, I'm sure you will." Amber smiled. Then she glanced at the men. "Are we going to be included, or not?"

Justin reached across the table and squeezed her hand. "You weren't including us."

"Woman-to-woman stuff." Amber chuckled.

After dinner, they climbed the stairs to the family room. Lori saw that Sean had now set up a computer and a large drafting table in the big room that overlooked the ski hills. Lights twinkled in the distance of the night as everyone pored over his house design.

"I like this a lot, Sean," Justin told him. "Have you had any luck finding a piece of land yet?"

Sean was close to Lori, their arms touching. He looked at her first before he said, "I haven't really looked. There hasn't been time."

Lori glanced at the large home he had designed. "Are you planning on building this?"

He nodded. "Either it or something similar eventually. This house is merely an investment, a stepping stone."

Amber laughed. "Sean wants to settle down and have a family. 'Cept we have to find him a wife first. He's fussy. We thought for sure he would get along with my cousin, Erica, at one time, but it didn't work out."

Lori forced a laugh. "I'm sure he'll soon meet someone willing to start his family and live in that lovely home."

Justin patted Sean on the back. "I'm sure he will. It's not you, obviously, Lori. Sean tells me you have plans to start your own firm before you get married. Are you going to stay in Ashton Heights?"

"Hopefully," she told him.

"I wish you good luck. It's hard work, but it's worth it."

They returned downstairs and sat around on the armchairs, talking. About half past eleven, Amber excused herself because she was tired. She said goodnight and went up to bed.

Justin rose as well. "Amber was going to tell you, but she's left it to me. We're going to have a baby."

Sean immediately got up and shook his friend's hand. "Congratulations. That's good news. I know you've both been wanting a baby."

Lori also shook Justin's hand. "Yes, congratulations. I hope everything works out."

"I do, too. Amber's pretty excited. Anyway, it's been wonderful meeting you, Lori. We'll see you again?"

"I'm sure I will," she said, wondering if she would. Sean might not invite her to meet his friends a second time.

When Justin was gone, Sean walked Lori home.

"Thank you very much," she told him. "I enjoyed the meal and the company. You're a good cook."

"I've learned to be. I've been a bachelor for a long time."

"You really do want to get married, don't you?"

He nodded. "Yes. I envy Justin and Amber their family way."

"I can tell you do," she said. "You should maybe give Amber's sister Erica another try."

"*Cousin* Erica," Sean said with a tight laugh. "She was a great woman, but we didn't match."

They had reached her front door. Lori asked. "So what constitutes a match?"

"Liking one another, friendship, compatibility, and being very much in love."

Lori pushed the key into the lock and opened it. Sean was behind her. Did he expect her to comment on his description of a match?

He laid his hand on her arm. "You really do want to wait for marriage, don't you?"

She nodded. "Yes. I do."

His hand dropped. "I'll say goodnight from here then."

Lori watched Sean walk back to his house, then she took off her coat, and went into the kitchen. She had enjoyed this evening. She had enjoyed the intimacy of two couples being together. One day, yes, she would like a marriage like Amber and Justin's. Amber was about two years older than Lori, and she was still young enough for a family. Lori was sure she had plenty of time. When she was settled in her career, she would find someone to love.

She heard the door open and Julie came home. Before she forgot, Lori told her sister about Janine's call.

"What kind of house extension does she want?" Julie asked. Fran had accosted Julie the minute she had walked through the door; now the cat ran around in a circle after some string Julie was trailing.

"A sun room. She saw Mom and Dad's."

"Yes, she did. She was enraptured. But why wait until next Saturday to see you. And why take Sean over?"

Lori had to come up with sufficient answers. She fibbed a bit. "Because she's hiring us through Randall & Rhodes, and because I won't be free until then. Neither will Sean."

Julie seemed to accept that explanation. "Okay. Next Saturday's fine with me. Did you know I was leaving next Monday?"

Lori pretended to be surprised. "No, I didn't."

"Yes. I've found a friend to stay with in the city, so I'm all set. You'll have your peace and quiet again."

Lori was surprised to feel so sad about that upcoming event. She thought she didn't want Julie around, but now she hated to see her leave again. "I'll miss you, Julie."

"I'll miss you as well, kid. It's been good being home again." Julie grinned. "Anyway, to bed. I have a heavy date tomorrow. Carson's coming into town."

"Carson Tyler from L.A.?"

"Same one."

"Where's he going to stay?"

"Up at the Hinton Lodge. We're going skiing. He's staying the weekend."

Julie didn't seem to want to say much more. Lori thought her sister seemed almost brittle this evening and wondered if it had anything to do with Carson. She had the impression Julie was in love with the man, but was fighting her love. Pretty much the same situation Lori had found herself in.

Carson arrived early on Saturday morning in a rented Mercedes. Lori had to entertain him in the kitchen while Julie got ready for a day on the slopes.

"Lots of snow here," Carson said as he sipped Lori's coffee. He was a tall, handsome man with black hair and a tan. He gave the appearance of being wealthy and successful—and he was.

"It's been snowing a lot; the slopes should be in good shape," Lori told him.

"Great." He glanced at the door, impatient for Julie to appear.

When she did, wearing a silver and blue ski suit, they left in the Mercedes. Lori put the answering machine to two rings and went upstairs to work.

Lori phoned Janine from the office on Monday morning to let her know that Julie had agreed to come on Saturday.

"She's curious, obviously, but she seems to accept the sun room story."

"Super," Janine said. "Just get her here."

Lori would definitely do that. She hung up the phone and began to settle to work.

"Lori."

She glanced up from her monitor. Sean, whom she hadn't seen since Friday evening, walked up to her desk. He carried some glossy pamphlets.

"I've been through these," he said. "And I've specified a couple of skylights we could use in our houses." He placed the pamphlets on the side of her desk. "Okay?"

She had completely forgotten about the skylights. She reached out and fingered the brochures. "Okay. I'll look through them."

He perched his hip on the corner of the desk. "I talked to your father. He's willing to give us an estimate, so he said he would drop by after work and have a look. All right?"

Lori frowned at him. "You talked to my father?"

"Yes. I called him about something else and I mentioned the skylights. He said he thought it was a great idea as he'd always thought your hallway was dark."

What else would Sean call her father about? They weren't near the construction stage of Hinton's yet. And everything else in the company had already been tendered. Her father was working on a housing tract close to Ellis Corners at the moment.

"Lori?" Sean prompted.

"Fine," she said. "Fine."

"Great. See you later."

Lori didn't dwell on the fact that their relationship hadn't progressed after his kiss. She would only make herself miserable if she allowed herself to think about him. Maybe, since she had made her point more than clear that she wasn't in the marriage market, he was now looking around for someone else to share his designer home.

Lori arrived home about the same time as her father's truck drew up at her curb. Her mother was with him. Alice, dressed in jeans and a quilted red bomber jacket, looked a bit like Julie. They both came into the house with Lori. Julie was there; Carson had flown home that morning.

"Great, you're here," Julie said, seeming to be her normal perky self. "Mom and Dad can stay for dinner.

I've made a huge pot of stew and I was going to freeze it for Lori so she will eat next week after I've gone, but you guys can have some."

Alice smiled at her elder daughter. "Sounds good and smells good. Shall we stay, Jack?"

"Oh, definitely." Jack was peering up at Lori's ceiling. "Is this where you want the skylight?"

"Yes. Just let me get out of my coat and I'll get the brochures Sean gave me."

Alice jogged her arm. "I want to meet Sean."

"Is that why you came with Dad?" Lori asked.

Alice grinned. "Of course not."

Lori laughed. "I'll go and phone him. I think he's home by now."

Lori managed to get her coat hung in the hall closet and went into the kitchen to phone Sean. Julie was stirring the stew on the stove. She had used a huge brand-new pot that Lori had never used before. *Which proves I never cook,* she thought, as she punched in Sean's phone number. While she listened to the rings, she observed her sister. Julie seemed to be much more active after being with Carson this weekend.

Her mother was fussing about cutlery and dishes for the upstairs dining room.

"Sean," she said when he answered.

"Invite him for dinner," Julie called out.

Lori made a face at her sister. "My Dad's here for the skylights. Do you want to come over?"

"Dinner," Julie mouthed and waved a spoon.

"And Julie wants you to come for dinner. She's made a stew thing."

"Thing?" he asked, sounding amused.

"Well, it's in a big pot and it smells good."

"I can smell it from here. I would love to have dinner with your family. I'll be there in five minutes."

Lori was checking the ceiling location for the skylight with her father when Sean arrived still wearing his slacks, shirt and tie from the office. Alice and Julie were handling the dinner arrangements but Alice immediately came by for an introduction.

"Pleased to meet you. I've heard about you from both the girls."

Sean laughed. "I seem to know them both from different eras."

"Coincidence," Alice said, and gave Lori a sideways glance. She raised her brows and rolled her eyes, which meant to Lori that her mother liked Sean.

"We'll go over to Sean's place and measure up there," Jack said. "I'll give you an estimate on labor." He winked. "We'll be competitive."

By the time they returned from Sean's house, the dinner was ready to eat in Lori's dining room. She hadn't formally used her dining room since her housewarming, when she had her Mom and Dad for dinner. She had to admit it was very pleasurable to have her family all together. She remembered when Julie had left home the first time to go to college and how she had cried because she missed her sister so much. She wouldn't cry this time, but Julie did complete the family picture. When she wasn't around, there was a void.

Sean fit in as well, but he seemed more interested in Julie this evening; giving her some hints on how to survive in Manhattan.

"We're a bit worried," Alice said.

"Mom, I lived in L.A. for four years. I'll be perfectly fine in New York."

"Yes, but your Dad's sister, Rachel, is in California. You had family."

"Aunt Rae was in Fresno, Mom. Miles away from where I was."

"But you had Carson as well."

"Mom. I'm staying with a girlfriend. I'll be fine."

"Well, I hope so. I'll worry anyway. I always do."

Julie shook her head. "Well, you've got a week left to not worry. I'm here until next Monday."

There was more consultation over the skylights after dinner before her parents left. Lori found that Sean and her Dad got along together really well. Actually, the three of them worked well together.

Sean stayed for another coffee to talk to Julie, then he went home as well. Lori went to bed. She lay awake staring at the ceiling until she fell asleep and dreamed of installing a skylight in every room in her ideal house.

Chapter Nine

Next Saturday evening, the night of Julie's surprise party, Lori wore jeans and a presentable white silk top. She packed her briefcase with sun room brochures, just to make it look as if she were really going to Janine's house to work. Sean had talked to her at the office on Friday about the party plans and he came over to her house about ten minutes before they were to leave.

Julie, wearing wide-legged black pants, a silver top, and her silver jacket, looked fine for a party. One thing about Julie: she always dressed in style. Lori didn't have to convince her to dress up and risk suspicion.

They drove over to Janine's in Sean's wagon. Lori let Julie sit in the front with Sean, even though Julie gave her a look when Lori jumped into the backseat.

Lori listened to Julie and Sean talk about old times all the way to the Fisher's house.

The house was a beautiful old brick home, still with Christmas decorations and lights around it. Even though the season was more than two months past, the glitter looked perfectly acceptable against the heaps of snow either side of the wide driveway. There weren't any other cars around. Lori presumed arrangements had been made with the neighbors for parking to hide vehicles.

Sean parked in the driveway and they walked to the front door. Sean pressed the doorbell and peered through the glass panel, then glanced at Lori and smiled slightly.

"I can't see that Janine needs any additions to this huge place," Julie said, tapping her booted foot impatiently. "Come on guys, it's freezing out here."

The door flung open, lights suddenly blazed.

"Surprise!" was yelled by a crowd, and Julie began to laugh.

"What have you done?" She looked at Lori and Sean. "You both knew about this?"

Lori smiled. "Yes, I knew." She placed her briefcase away in a corner. She was sure there would be no discussion of the sun room tonight, even though Janine really did want one.

Howard came over to Sean and the two men high-fived.

"Great to see you again, Matheson." Howard looked

at Lori. "Small world, isn't it? You working with Sean, while he's our good buddy."

"Very small world," Lori agreed.

Janine had a huge spread of food in the dining room and they picked up some food and drinks. Sean had a lot of friends to reacquaint himself with, so Lori sat and chatted to Janine and one of Janine's neighbors while she ate. Howard had put on some music and people were starting to dance. Julie was with a dark-haired man Lori didn't recognize.

She was standing at the edge of the crowd, wondering if she could escape now she had done her duty and brought Julie here, when Sean came over to her.

"Do you want to dance?" he asked.

She did, but she shouldn't. Sean had her in the typical confused mess she was usually in when he was around. "Well, I suppose, but I haven't danced since college."

"Too busy working hard?"

She nodded. "Probably."

"I know what you mean. I haven't really danced much over the past few years. But we can tonight."

As Lori matched Sean's fast, uninhibited steps to the popular music, she remembered her first impression of him when she had seen him in his black suit and overcoat. That Monday he had been an immaculately dressed architect. This Saturday he was a young man having fun. And she was having fun as well. She loved dancing with him. When the music slowed in pace, they moved together and his kiss seemed natural.

When he raised his head, he said, "This has been coming between us from day one, Lori."

Even though her heart was beating rapidly, she acted coy. "Now what are you talking about?"

His arms tightened around her back. "Us."

She put her arms around his neck. "You and me, like?"

"Yes. That's what I mean." He pulled her close to him and she felt his mouth linger in her hair. "I wanted this from the moment I first saw you."

So had she. But she had fought it. She was still going to fight it. She had her plans. She wasn't going to back down just because she was in a dark soulful atmosphere with Sean. She needed to be somewhere brilliantly-lit with him.

She tugged away from him, although she couldn't seem to disentangle herself from his arms and still had her hands loosely linked at his neck. "I need a drink of water, Sean."

He let her go then. "All right. Let's go find the kitchen."

They walked hand-in-hand from the rocking room and walked across the hallway to the kitchen. Janine's son, Jake, was in his pajamas eating a peanut butter sandwich.

"Are they starving you?" Lori asked as she ran the tap water cold to get a drink.

Jake screwed up his nose. "I don't like all that fancy food stuff."

"It would probably give you indigestion anyway. So how's school?"

"Fine."

Sean handed her a glass from an assortment on a tray.

"Thanks," she told him. "Do you know Sean Matheson, Jake?"

"No."

"Well, this is Sean. He's an architect, the same as me."

Sean shook Jake's hand politely.

"Pleased to meet you Jake," Sean said. "Where did you get that peanut butter?"

"You want a sandwich?"

"I wouldn't mind."

Lori laughed. "I'll have one, too, if you have some strawberry jelly to put on it."

Jake got all the fixings from the refrigerator. Lori and Sean made their sandwiches and then sat at the kitchen table to eat them. Jake sat with them, acting as if they were all doing something conspiratorial. Lori started him talking about hockey. It turned out Sean was a hockey fan and the two got on well. When they were finished eating, Jake scampered back to bed with a glass of milk.

"We'll get him in bad habits," Lori commented.

Sean nodded and looked a little pensive.

Lori licked some jelly from her fingers.

"Do you think Ken would mind if we dated?" Sean asked.

The question seemed out of the blue, but shouldn't have been unexpected after their earlier conversation. She shook her head. "Not really. His wife and kids have all worked around the office at one time or another. But it doesn't really matter what Ken thinks. I don't want to date a guy in the office, Sean."

"What have we been doing then? I mean, we went to the ice sculptures, you came to dinner, we're here this evening."

"Only because you moved in almost next door to me and Julie happened to know you."

"Not because we work together, or that we've been interested in one another from the first time we met?"

"You know my philosophy, Sean. You want more than me, and it's not fair for me to hang around with you and give you any false hope."

He stared at her for a long moment, as if he hadn't heard her, then he rose from his chair and placed it beneath the table in a neat but definite manner. "I know you don't know the meaning of the word, but I'm going to have some *fun.*"

He strode out of the kitchen. Lori shut her eyes for a moment to try and stop the tears from blurring her vision. This is what you want, Lori. So why should it hurt so badly?

She managed to keep on the periphery of the party

for the rest of the evening. Sean was dancing with a
bold redhead in flared jeans and a skimpy blue
sweater; he seemed to be having the fun he wanted.

That woman could be you, Lori.

Eventually, she told Janine she had a headache and
called a taxi to take her home.

When she went to tell Julie she was leaving early,
her sister frowned. "Lori, what about Sean?"

"He's found his fun."

"But earlier you two looked like you were having
a great time. I saw you—"

"We discussed things and it's better this way. So
I'll see you later, Julie."

"Take care," Julie said. "I worry about you."

Fran cuddled up on the bed with her that night but
Lori couldn't sleep. She thought she was waiting for
Julie to come in, but even when Julie was in bed, she
still didn't sleep. *Had she done the right thing with
Sean?*

She knew she would find out the answer to her
question on Monday morning at work. She had probably severely strained relations with Sean.

Julie was leaving mid-morning on Monday. Lori
hugged her sister before she left for work.

"I really will miss you."

"You can come to New York and visit me. It's not
as far away as L.A."

"Maybe I will do that," Lori told her. And she meant it. Maybe she should get away from Ashton Heights, from Sean.

"Are you going to keep Fran?"

Lori glanced at the little cat sitting, watching them. "Yes. I think I will."

"Good. Mother needs a home for her. This will be perfect."

Lori waved Julie goodbye. Then she gathered her briefcase and drove to work. She discovered that Sean wasn't in today. She would have to wait another day and night to feel the consequences of her actions on Saturday evening.

At noon, on her way out to lunch, Lori asked Mary where Sean was.

"New York City to see a client."

"What client?"

Mary frowned. "He didn't say exactly, but he called earlier for messages."

Lori went home that evening feeling as if she had the entire weight of the world on her shoulders. The house was silent without Julie. She had to cook herself a meal. She made do with an omelet and salad.

Her father phoned to say he couldn't get the skylights until next week, so he would begin the installation then. It didn't matter if it was put off a week, did it?

"No. It doesn't matter, Dad." Lori told him. She didn't want to do the skylights now. She didn't want to deal with Sean. She was sure he was really mad at her. Or possibly she had hurt him. He wasn't one of those men who didn't admit to being upset or hurt. It's one of the things she liked about him.

Sean wasn't at work on Tuesday either.

"Sean's still in New York," Mary told her before Lori had a chance to ask. "He'll be back tomorrow morning."

"Fine." She flipped her hair over the shoulders of her black suit jacket. "I really don't care."

Mary gave her a knowing look. "Then why do you look so miserable?"

Lori explained that her sister had been staying and now she was gone.

"If you insist that's the reason, I'll accept it," Mary told her.

Lori couldn't argue that she didn't care about Sean. Because she *did* care about Sean. She had to admit she was so much in love with him, she ached. Is this how he had felt about his ex-girlfriend? Love wasn't worth this pain, was it?

She knew she had to get a life. So she phoned Susan when she got home. Susan said she had a date.

"I've met this really nice guy," Susan said.

"How long have you been dating him?"

"One whole week and four hours. We seem made for one another."

"Are you in love?" Lori asked. Susan was her last single girlfriend.

"Yes. His name is David and he's already talking about getting married. I'll let you meet him soon. Maybe we can double date—He's got a groovy friend."

"I don't think so, Susan." Lori blurted out her problem. "I went and fell in love with Sean Matheson, the architect."

"Is that a problem? Doesn't he like you?"

"Yes. I think he likes me, but he won't wait for me."

"You mean, you really would make a guy wait? Are you crazy?"

"I think I might be. He wanted to date me, but I turned that down."

"Lori!"

"He doesn't fit in with my plans, Susie. He's too soon."

"Lori, don't be so rigid. Give a little."

"I think I've lost my chance now."

"You're nuts."

"I'll get over it."

"I don't think you ever get over being that nuts."

Lori laughed. "You're always around to cheer me up. Anyway, have a nice time this evening. We'll get together some other time."

"If you make up with Sean, let me know, and we'll do that double date."

"All right," Lori said, but she knew she wouldn't

be making anything up with Sean. There was nothing to make up.

She was amazed at love, at the way pain turned to excitement when she remembered she'd be seeing Sean on Wednesday. She hummed a pop song as she dressed in a new dark blue wool dress and jacket, clothes she hadn't worn to the office yet. *This is crazy,* she thought as she drove to work in light snow. *I feel as if I'm on an out-of-control carnival ride.*

Sean's wagon was already parked in his space. Lori hurried through the door.

"He's here," Mary said.

"I know," Lori said breathlessly.

"He's in with Ken and Peter."

"That's fine." She picked up her messages, and Mary handed her a courier package that had come in for her.

Bob and Alan were chatting in the main office. They seemed happy about something.

"What's up?" she asked.

Bob grinned. "Matheson's come through with a huge multi-million-dollar shopping center to be built right here on the outskirts of Ashton Heights."

Lori stopped in her tracks. "A shopping center."

"That's what we've heard. Great news. I was thinking none of the firm's jobs were going to come through and there might be some slow time this spring, but now we're going to be busy."

Feeling slightly dazed by the news, Lori went

through to her office. She hung up her coat. What did this mean?

It means, Lori, that Sean has just brought a multi-million-dollar job into the firm. He's on his way to promotion. He's going to be a big wheel sooner than you thought.

Big city architect, she thought, slumping in her chair, feeling like a deflated balloon. He probably had this job contact in the works since he arrived. He had probably used the shopping center as a tool to get Randall & Rhodes to hire him. No wonder he let you have free reign on Hinton's. It wasn't a big enough job to worry about. Now he'll be overseeing the shopping center, a really major project. And you'll be in your little corner, not even a real office, working on your little ski resort.

"Lori?" It was Sean, wearing his black slacks, black shirt and silver tie. "How are you?"

She forced a bright smile. "I'm fine. Why?"

"You left early on Saturday evening."

She meant to say she had been tired, but she said what came to her lips. "Well, I'm not much fun, am I?"

He came closer. "I'm sorry I said that."

"It's true."

"No. It's not true. We were having fun before we had that chat in the kitchen."

"Were we?"

She saw his jaw tighten up. "I thought we were.

That's why...." He rubbed his jaw. "We'll have to talk later."

She shook her head. "I think we said it all, Sean. Let's leave it. And congratulations on the shopping center. Ashton Heights needs a decent mall."

"Thank you. I'm proud to bring such a big project into the practice."

"I'm sure you are. You'll be busy."

He nodded. "Yes, I will be very busy. You might have to help out on the job."

"Really?"

"Unless we hire some more staff. We'll see." He backed out of her office. "See you later, Lori."

Lori glared after him. No way was she going to work as part of a team on a huge job. She liked the little individual jobs best. That way she got more design control. There was really no solution to this problem, but to get into her own business as soon as possible.

Lori's goals felt more imperative in the next few days. The buzz over the mall had certainly squeezed her project into a small space. Sean even had his photo in the small community paper, along with Ken and Peter, detailing the size of the project and showcasing Randall & Rhodes.

Lori was convinced that Sean had known all along he was bringing the mall into the firm; letting her have full control of Hinton's had been excellent strategy to make her feel good.

Except she didn't feel good. Oh, she liked heading the project. Alan was a pleasure to work with; he didn't seem to mind taking instructions from her and he was astute, with good ideas of his own. George was easygoing. Everything was fine, except. . . .

Except what, Lori?

Except she was in love with Sean. She had feared falling in love with him even before she had met him, which was why she had been so full of trepidation that first day. She should have turned around in the snowstorm like she had wanted to and not come into work. Instead, she had fallen in love with him from day one.

She shook her head and let her eyes focus on her computer screen once more. But she didn't want love, did she? She had told everyone love could wait.

Love is urgent.

Even her house felt lonely now. If it weren't for Fran she would feel really terrible. One thing she didn't do: She didn't watch Sean's house. That would only be torturing herself. Although sometimes she couldn't help see his light burning upstairs in the family room where he had his home office.

Lori had to extricate herself from her current misery. Therefore, she put the wheels in motion for her own business, and went to look at office space. One office was in downtown Ashton Heights. It was a room above a pet food store and looked out over the back lane where the trucks made deliveries to the store. But the rent was expensive for the location and type of office it was. The other was just out of town in a new office block. But the rents were astronomical. She could work from home, she supposed, but she was a little off the beaten track in the residential area. Finally she found a room in a commercially-zoned house on the way downtown. The rent was reasonable and the space wouldn't be fully decorated and available until mid-summer. Other small businesses were moving in at that time as well. She would have time to finish Hinton's Ski Lodge and hand in her resignation with time to spare. She might even find a job to start off her new firm.

One job she went after was Janine and Howard Fisher's sun room. She went and met with them on Friday evening to discuss their ideas and came away with enough information to work on some plans for them.

On Saturday her father came over to her house to install her skylight.

"I did Sean's," he told her. "It looks good."

"That's nice." She didn't want to be reminded of Sean. Sean had disrupted her entire life.

When her father was finished, Lori helped him clean up.

"Sean and Ken have mentioned a shopping center job," Jack told Lori. "I'll probably tender for the job. Are you going to work on it?"

"No, I'm not. I'm getting out of there quickly." She

explained that she had found an office space to rent in the summer.

Jack frowned. "Are you ready for this move, Lori?"

"Sure, I am. I've got my first job for Lori Fenton, Architect, AIA: Janine and Howard Fisher's sun room."

"You'll need more than that small job to keep a business going."

"I know. But I'll find some work."

Jack shook his head. "I thought you were thrilled that you had a ski resort under your wing."

"I only have the ski resort under my wing because Mr. Sean "Super Architect" Matheson, had a shopping mall in the works. But he didn't think to mention that."

"Lori," her father soothed. "Don't be like that. Ken wasn't having much much luck around here. He has to keep the firm going, Sweetie. And Sean has to look out for his job as well. No work, and he's out as well."

"I know, Dad. But *I'm* going out on my own."

"Things haven't worked out with Sean?"

"It has nothing to do with Sean. I've had these plans forever. And now I'm going to institute them."

"All right. Well, you know I'm behind you all the way. Just don't do anything rash."

Lori helped her father put his tools in the truck. Then she waved him goodbye. She scooped up Fran by the door and cuddled the cat. She had already done something rash. She had fallen in love with Sean. But she was on her way to overcoming that obstacle.

Chapter Ten

Sunday was bright and sunny. Lori worked on Janine and Howard's sun room for awhile, then talked to Julie on the phone.

"I'm sure you would love living here," Julie raved. "You could groove around the Guggenheim for hours. Wasn't it designed by a famous architect?"

"Frank Lloyd Wright," Lori said. "Actually, I'm not doing too badly. I'm working on the sun room for Janine and Howard, away from the office, and I've found a space to rent to go out on my own by the summer."

"You're going out on your own right away? What brought that on? You're not running away from Sean, I hope."

Lori wouldn't admit it, if she was. In her mind she

was protecting her career. This had nothing to do with loving Sean. "No. The situation at work isn't really what I want anymore, so I think I'll make the move earlier."

"I wish you luck, Lori. I'm sure you'll be successful. You're so determined."

After Lori had finished talking to Julie, she couldn't concentrate on the sun room drawings anymore. She dressed in old jeans and a denim jacket, and went outside to clip some dead shrubs and think about her spring landscaping.

She was raking some dead grass from her lawn when Sean came by in his wagon. He slowed down, and stopped by her driveway with the engine still running.

"Hi. Nice weather?"

She shaded her eyes with her hand. "Very nice."

"How's it going?"

"Great. How's it going with you?"

"Fine, Lori." He took the wagon out of gear and started moving again. "See you around."

"Yes. Bye."

Lori returned to attacking her lawn.

In the morning Lori arrived at work at the same time as Sean. He must take a different route from her, she thought, because she never saw him leave his house nor met him on the road.

"Did you get your lawn raked?" he asked.

"Yes, I did."

"I thought the maintenance agreement took care of it."

"It does, but I like to do some gardening myself."

They reached the door. Sean opened it for her and stood to one side to let her through. Lori grabbed her messages and took off to her office. This was a terrible situation. But it was only for another few months and then she would be free.

Sean followed her into her office. "Lori."

She unbuttoned her cream trenchcoat. "What, Sean?"

He glanced behind him, then moved further into her office. "Do you want to go for lunch at The Heights?"

She hadn't been to The Heights since she went with Julie and discovered Sean was more of a local than she had thought. Common sense told her to say no. But then she thought about the long-term consequences of being on bad terms with Sean who might one day be her sole competition in town. That might be suicide to her own practice. Ashton Heights was such a small place. Sean only had to put in the word that she was difficult to deal with and she wouldn't get any business.

"Well?" he said impatiently.

"All right. Fine. One o'clock?"

"Great. After lunch I want to show you a building site."

"Another big project you've got up your sleeve?" She couldn't help the sarcasm.

"Ah, Lori," he said. "Is this what your cold shoulder is all about?"

"I've been busy Sean. We're at work when we're in this building."

"I understand that, but we've also had some pleasant times together. I thought we were at least friends, even if you didn't want any more than that."

"Sean. It doesn't make any sense to pretend something that isn't there."

He moved closer. "But there is something there. That's the problem, Lori. *There is.*" He raked his hand through his hair. "Okay. I'll see you at one by the door. We'll sort this out."

Lori wished she could leave this week, but she couldn't, so she supposed she did have to sort out her relationship with Sean.

One o'clock finally came and Lori met Sean by the door. His spring black leather jacket had no lining and he wore it over a white long-sleeved shirt and black tie. She thought his hair was a little longer than when he had arrived, and he also seemed thinner somehow. Maybe his face was more gaunt. She couldn't quite figure out what it was about him that appeared different.

At The Heights they chose a booth and settled down with menus. After they had ordered the soup and sandwich special, Sean leaned over the table.

"Is there anything missing from your life, Lori?"

It was a question she hadn't expected. She wasn't

sure what she had expected, but she knew this lunch wasn't about work—not after what he had said in her office.

She couldn't tell the truth. "There's nothing missing."

"Oh." He ran his fingers across his jaw in a weary gesture. "There's a lot missing from mine. For one, I miss what we had when I first arrived."

Her heart began to beat again. Had it not been beating over the last few weeks? She moistened her lips with her tongue. "What did we have?"

"A rapport."

Lori sipped some water to try and keep her mouth from drying up. "We were working on the same job at that time. Now we're not. That's what you intended, didn't you?"

His forehead creased. "I'm not following you."

Lori realized that if she didn't come clean with Sean, if she just harbored her feelings, she wasn't ever going to feel good again. "You knew you were getting that shopping center job, that's why you handed me the full reins on the ski resort."

"I didn't know I was getting the mall then, Lori. I had contacted the client about a year ago when I was getting bored with my other position. But the client never got back to me, so I thought it was a dead deal. Half the reason I came back to this area was job dissatisfaction. Coming here seemed to clinch the deal because the client was looking for the right location and Ashton Heights happened to be perfect. I handed you the reins on the ski resort because I could see I wasn't really needed. You were quite capable of heading the project."

"What would you have done if the mall hadn't come in?"

He shrugged. "I'm not so sure. I gave up the ski resort before the mall was confirmed."

"You mean, you would have lost your job because of me?"

"I can always go somewhere else, but you can't Lori. This is where you want to be, where you want to open your first company. I understand that."

Impulsively, Lori reached her hand across the table between their coffee cups and glasses of water. "That was taking a chance."

"Maybe it was." Sean squeezed her fingers and they remained holding hands until their meals arrived.

When they had eaten, Sean drove out on the road toward Hinton's Ski Lodge. He turned onto a back road that wound down to the river. A couple of new houses had been built along the road, but he stopped at an empty lot.

They walked up the hillside to a view of rolling hills and trees.

Sean stood beside her with his hands shoved in his jacket pockets. "Remember that house I was designing?"

Lori nodded. "Is this where you're going to build it?"

"Eventually, I hope. The land is for sale."

"Then you're considering buying it?"

He nodded.

"I would. It's beautiful out here."

Sean was looking at her very intensely.

"Julie phoned me yesterday," he said. "She said you had found an office space and would be leaving Randall & Rhodes in the summer."

"Yes, that's right. I'm working on it."

"That cuts down on two years, Lori."

She nodded. "Yes. It does."

"Then will you look over my house design and put in your own ideas?"

Lori pushed aside a lock of hair that was blowing in the breeze. "As a job for my new firm?"

"Yes." He swallowed hard. "I want you to make it *our* house, Lori."

"Sean—"

"I really don't care if I'm making a fool of myself, but I love you, Lori. I want to marry you. I want to live with you. Here."

She was flown away. It was so out of the blue. Or was it? They had developed a rapport—more than a rapport. They had both felt the chemistry, she had never really doubted that. She swallowed hard. She loved him, but . . . "But my practice, my plans. Even though I'm starting earlier, it will take some time to work up the business."

He moved a step closer on the grass. "Are you saying you love me?"

She couldn't fib. "Yes. I love you, Sean. I think I did from day one, but—"

He sighed with relief and then said, "You have these plans, you have these goals, you have life designed, all figured out. Yes. I know. But I'm not waiting, Lori. I'll give you until the weekend to decide what you want to do."

He began to stride down the slope. Lori followed him. "You can't give me just a few days to decide whether I want to marry now instead of later."

He swiveled around. "Yes, I can. I've had it with waiting all my life. I want to rush into this. I want us to arrange a wedding and build this house. You can still have your business. We'll just be married, that's all."

"What about you?"

"What about me? I have a job, a promise of a partnership. I'm fine. I'll survive."

He began walking again. They reached the wagon and climbed in. The trip back to the office was heavy.

"What do we do with our two houses?" Lori asked at last.

"Sell them, combine the profits, and use them to build the new home. You can probably use some of the money for your new office space as well."

"You have it all worked out."

"I've been working it out since Ken's party."

"Is that when you. . . ."

"Decided I was in love with you? No."

Lori frowned. "When then?"

"Remember the day you came into work that first week and we ordered pizza?"

She nodded. "Yes, I remember."

"I knew that day that I had fallen in love with you. You were wondering if I was worried about working with you because you were a woman. I was only worried because I knew I was in love with you."

"Other than. . . ." she said softly.

" 'I'm in love with you,' was the rest of the sentence."

He drove into the office parking lot and slipped the wagon into a space. "Now you've heard my feelings. I would like to have ended up kissing you but obviously that's not what you want. You want a more lonely life than I do."

He left her to make her way out by herself. He was already halfway into his office when she reached the front door. Mary glanced at her.

"Are you all right, Lori?"

"I'm fine," she said, and forced a smile.

In her office, she sat staring out of the window. The trees were budding, some shrubs even had fresh green leaves on them. What was more important, she wondered. Was it love? Or was it career? She had always thought it was career, but now she wasn't sure she was right. She longed to be held in Sean's arms. She imagined living in a house they co-designed on that beautiful piece of land. She imagined being married to Sean. And the vision seemed so right.

She placed her elbows on her desk and her face in her hands. What should she do? If she gave up Sean, she might never love again. This might be her only chance. And she really wouldn't be giving up her plans. She already had her office space marked. She would have capital from her house sale to help as well. Things might actually be easier, be better. Except she might have to compromise more with a husband, and maybe even a child.

Did she want it all?

It was a question that went home with her, a question that she fretted over for the rest of the week, a question she had until the weekend to answer.

A freak snowstorm covered the state below Lake Ontario on Saturday morning. Lori woke up to howling winds and a world of white. She glanced out of the window and saw Sean's kitchen lights were on. How did he expect them to get together this weekend to talk about his proposition? Would he phone and demand a meeting, much like he had demanded that lunch at The Heights?

She couldn't wait for that. She was sick of analyzing everything. She needed to see him, needed to act. She wanted to be with him now.

Not thinking of the consequences of what she was doing, Lori fed Fran and dressed up in her quilted jacket and a pair of high boots. With her hands rattling her keys in her pocket, she trudged over to Sean's house.

He must have seen her coming up the drive, because the door opened before she had a chance to knock or ring the doorbell.

"This is a late April surprise," he said with a smile. "And so are you."

"We seem to meet in snowstorms," Lori told him and returned his smile. *Could she live without his smile for the rest of her life?*

"I'll make hot chocolate. You like it, don't you? I remember you had some at Mom's house."

Lori hung up her jacket and took off her boots. She glanced up at the skylight that was blocked with snow. "It doesn't do much good in this weather," she said. "But it is brighter."

"It is. Even covered with snow. Come through to the kitchen."

She pattered through in her socked feet. He was cooking bacon and eggs.

"Wonderful," she said. "A good dose of fat."

"I know, but it seems like the type of morning for good old-fashioned unhealthy food. Besides I needed cheering up."

"Are you miserable?"

"Yes. I'm miserable, because I know you've come to tell me we can't get engaged."

"Not necessarily," Lori said, but she knew she couldn't string him along. She had to be truthful. She stuffed her hands into the back pockets of her jeans. "I do love you, Sean. I do want to be engaged to you. I really like that piece of land."

He gave her a long hard look. "But?"

"But I made all these plans." She withdrew her hands from her pockets and began to pace his kitchen tiles. "I wanted to be Ashton Heights' first woman architect. I wanted to do it on my own, without help from a husband or anyone. I wanted—"

"To be alone," he said and turned to the stove to lower the heat beneath the frying pan.

"Yes. I wanted to be alone. I left home because I wanted to be alone. Then when Julie came to stay, I didn't want that. I didn't want the cat."

He eyed her sideways. "But you kept the cat?"

"Yes. I kept the cat. I couldn't let her go. And I miss Julie. I don't like it alone quite so much anymore."

"Do I come into this 'not liking it alone so much?' I mean, since you met me, have you been thinking about things?"

She nodded. "Yes. I've been thinking about things. I've been fighting loving you."

"Could you compromise?"

Lori nodded slowly. "I think I might have to."

He turned the stove right off and came over to her. "I'm going to kiss you, Lori, but only if it's the real thing."

Her mouth trembled for his kiss, her arms longed to hold him. She put all thoughts of her career out of her mind. She would deal with it later, during her life with Sean. After all, she had dealt with the rest of her life in the midst of her crazy family, hadn't she?

"It's the real thing," she said.

He put his arms around her and pulled her to him. His kiss was gentle and warm. "I think we're going to have a nice cozy weekend designing our house," he said softly.

"You know," she told him, stroking back his hair from his face. "You came along and wrecked my life's design."

Sean smiled. "Try designing your life around love instead."

"I will," she said. "I'll begin today."